The Roving Sh

THE
SEAGULL
LIBRARY OF
FRENCH
LITERATURE

The Roving Shadows

PASCAL QUIGNARD

TRANSLATED BY CHRIS TURNER

LONDON NEW YORK CALCUTTA

Seagull Books, 2024

Originally published in French as Pascal Quignard,
Les Ombres errantes
© Éditions Grasset & Fasquelle, 2002

First published in English by Seagull Books, 2011
English translation © Chris Turner, 2010

ISBN   978 1 8030 9 365 9

British Library Cataloguing-in-Publication Data
A catalogue record for this book is available
from the British Library

Typeset and designed by Seagull Books, Calcutta, India
Printed and bound by WordsWorth India, New Delhi, India

CONTENTS

Chapter 1 (The Young German Woman)   1

Chapter 2 (The Shadow of Sexual Bliss)   5

Chapter 3 (The *tertium*)   11

Chapter 4 (Buddhas of Bamiyan)   12

Chapter 5 Nordstrand   15

Chapter 6 (We)   21

Chapter 7 The Nursling   22

Chapter 8 (Last Kingdom)   26

Chapter 9 The Ewer   34

Chapter 10 (The Absent One)   38

Chapter 11 Cras   39

Chapter 12 (The Horse)   42

Chapter 13 The Bark   43

Chapter 14 (The Dark Sky)   45

Chapter 15 Shadows   46

Chapter 16 List from the Year 2001   55

Chapter 17 (Television)   57

Chapter 18 On the Arrest of Monsieur de
              Saint-Cyran on 14 May 1638   59

Chapter 19 (Pluto)   61

Chapter 20 (Mogador)   74

Chapter 21 The Snuffers   75

Chapter 22 (Ubi)   82

Chapter 23 (The Region of Dawn)   83

Chapter 24 (Dawn Mist)   87

Chapter 25 (Banks of the Yonne)   89

Chapter 26 The Immortal King of the Ages   91

Chapter 27 Saint Bartholomew's Day   95

Chapter 28 Last Farewell   105

Chapter 29 Han Yu   107

Chapter 30 The Vestals   114

Chapter 31 (Mud)   117

Chapter 32 Churches of Leyden   118

Chapter 33 Post tenebras   119

Chapter 34 Perditos   128

Chapter 35 (The Keep at Vincennes)   129

Chapter 36 The Barefoot Teacher   130

Chapter 37 Terror   131

Chapter 38 (The Bassin du Roi at Le Havre)   136

Chapter 39 (Saint-Cyran)   137

Chapter 40 (Lancelot)   149

Chapter 41 (Monsieur de Merveilleux)   150

Chapter 42 The *Brouette*   151

Chapter 43 (Monasteries)   154

Chapter 44 (Going from Bergheim to Frankfurt)   162

Chapter 45 (Dream)   173

Chapter 46 (The Hunter)   175

Chapter 47 Emily   183

Chapter 48 History   185

Chapter 49 (Right of Asylum)   186

Chapter 50 (Shoreline)   196

Chapter 51 On the River that Flows into
              the Flowers   197

Chapter 52 (Marc Antoine Charpentier)   205

Chapter 53 The Other Kingdom   208

Chapter 54 (Kingdom of Jerusalem)   214

Chapter 55 Sofiius' End   215

Translator's Notes   226

CHAPTER 1

The crowing of the cockerel, the dawn, the barking of dogs, the gathering daylight, a man rising, nature, time, dreams, lucidity—everything is fierce.

I cannot touch the coloured covers of certain books without feeling a painful sensation rise within me.

A body once liked reading them better than it liked me. A young German woman looked after me until I was two. The fact that she read by my side robbed me of the joy of being near her, because it seemed then that she wasn't at my side. She wasn't there. She was already gone.

She was elsewhere.

In her reading, she inhabited another kingdom.

My throat suddenly tightens, bringing back those hours when I couldn't yet speak. They mask another world that will always elude my questing. My upper body was choked by a sort of dry sob.

I couldn't swallow.

I couldn't bear to have a fork or spoon come near my lips.

The attraction books exert on me is of a kind that will be more mysterious and imperious my whole life long than it may seem to other readers. Quickly, quickly, I put the old coloured book back whence I took it. I turn away from the bookseller's stall. I cannot speak, as was the way then. I dare not venture to. I hurry along the pavement, moving off into the shadows of the town, melting into them.

*

A piece of the original apple has remained stuck in the middle of my throat.

*

Old bilingual Latin-French Garnier editions grown downy with use, age, sun and dust.

I read in one of these old Garnier books that the emperor Tiberius insisted on having entirely yellow cylinders with no *tituli* on them for storing the scrolls of pornographic images he collected, so that nothing should betray the curiosity that obsessed him.

He wandered around the empire he was escaping.

A reviled emperor, a wolf, hating towns and cities, wanting nothing of the empire, an emperor who killed God and fled Rome itself.

He preferred to live at the highest point on Capri, in the shadow of the rock jutting out over the sea.

*

To live hidden—Lucretius' Latin word was *late*.

Larvatus, said Descartes.[†]

*

It happened that in 1618 the Chevalier Le Cerf, while barely yet out of his childhood, enlisted as a volunteer in the royal army, with the aim of travelling all over the world.

He joined William the Silent's troops at the Siege of Breda.

He stayed for thirteen months.

Four men became friends. They were four bar-rack-room companions, in order of enlistment: Monsieur de Jaume, René Des Cartes, Nathan Le Cerf, Isaac Beeckman. On the Day of the Barricades, 27 August 1648, Des Cartes brought forward his departure from Paris, with the result that he was unable to meet either Le Cerf, who went by the nick-name 'Abraham', or Jacques Esprit. He jumped on his horse. Arriving in Leyden, he said he would never again return to France. On 31 March 1649,[†] Chevalier Des Cartes wrote to Chanut: 'I have reason to believe they want me back in France only to show me off as though I were a panther.' He confesses he was nostalgic for the little house near the church beside the Western canal (*in den Westerheerckstraet*). It was in that year that he gave up the sexual favours of Frantsinge. But one cannot deduce from a life which becomes entirely hidden that it is more innocent.

CHAPTER 2

I seek only thoughts that tremble. There is a flush that belongs to the interior of the soul. The sixth book of the *Chin P'ing Mei* (*The Plum in the Golden Vase*)[†] sees the sudden appearance of the scholar Wen Pi'ku. He isn't yet forty. His dress and hair are those of a scholar; he has white teeth, side-whiskers, whiskers on his chin and on his lip. Hsi-men Ch'ing greets him. He takes him up to the reception hall. He has him sit down. He offers him a drink, then eventually bows to him:

'What is your name?'

Wen Pi'ku replies:

'My humble forename is *Pi'ku* (Need-to-Imitate-the-Ancients). My personal name is *Ri-hsin* (Renew-Oneself-Day-by-Day).

They drink tea by the light of a torch.

*

Such is the double bind of the scholar's name. I renew myself day by day in the need to imitate the works of the Ancients.

*

The name Wen Pi'ku reminds us of Lao-Tzu's: Lao (old) and Tzu (child). The scholar is by turns a Child of Old Parents and an Old Child.

The ancient Chinese tell that Lao-Tzu waited eighty years in his mother's womb before making up his mind to come out into the air and the light.

Lao-Tzu is clearly a *viviparus*.

*

There is a life before birth which dates it.

There is a world before the world into which it emerges.

There is a *foetus* before the *infans*.

There is an *infans* before the *puer*.

There is, unceasingly, a languageless 'before' to time: it is time.

Foetus, *infans*, before identity, are both without language.

*

The scene in which every scene has its origin in languageless invisibility is a ceaselessly active actuality.

*

After introducing himself, Wen Pi'ku murmurs to Hsi-men Ch'ing:

'When, at times, I weary of wandering in the forest of brushes and among the streams of ink, I take off my four-cornered hat and leave the smell of old books behind me. My hand slips beneath my silk trousers. I close my eyes. The tears of the god spurt forth. I bend my nostrils to the odour of the Erstwhile. This is the life that I lead.'

*

Three golden hairs belong to the devil.[†] The hero goes down to hell.

*

The most distant past is densest with explosive energy. Every intense memory comes close to force.

*

It is one thing to reason, quite another to see and to report one's vision in a book. In the Saint Joseph Monastery at Avila, Theresa said: 'Desire must not be purged of the bodily or involuntary images that fuel it.'

*

Every shadow that envelops our bodies is that of the scene that never comes into view, since it is the scene that is at our origins.

We could neither hear nor see those who made us, nor what made us, nor how it was done, before we *were*. It happens that human beings forget that they *are* not, before being.

But we lie: we always believe we heard something in the shadows, before being subject to the atmospheric air, before our eyes were opened to the light of the sun.

We were constructed in the shadows. Passively in the shadows. We are the fruits of the lidless ear of the shadows.

*

In umbra voluptatis lusi.

I have played in the shade of pleasures.

This expression, simple as it is, comes from Petronius.[†]

We should translate it even more precisely to say, I have played in the *shade of sexual bliss*.

*

In umbra voluptatis.

The shade of pleasure. When we are born we are still *shades of pleasure.*

De vita contemplativa: the cradle. Inactive. Barely having lungs. Tight and hunched in our nudity.

In the mythology of the ancient Etruscans this is Tages, the child-sized, grey-haired sage.

King of the last kingdom.

Tages the mute, *infans* king, who left books behind him: the *Libri Tagetici.*

CHAPTER 3

It is a property of the structure of language that it is its own *tertium*.

The writer, like the thinker, knows who is the real narrator within him: formulation.

This is what I do: the work of language weighing, thinking, inclining, expending itself.

CHAPTER 4

Dawn broke suddenly, rapidly. All at once it scattered its flecks of gold on the rims of the clouds, on the hilltops, the treetops, on the roiling waters of the streams. All at once, everything awoke. They too. They too shivered. They got up at that point too.

On Sunday, 7 December 1941, the day the Christians draw near to their idol to express their love of God, after dawn had broken, 188 bombers arrived on the Hawaiian coast.

They overflew the bay of Pearl Harbor. They sank 18 ships, destroyed 357 planes, killed 2,403 men.

Those overcome by fear could move neither their hands nor their feet. They remained speechless.

They teetered on the edge of destruction.

*

Two towers taller than the Tower of Babel collapsed *exactly like the great stone Buddhas of Bamiyan.*

*

The first world-scale civil war.

*

Your step began to totter: *labavit gressus.*[†] Your sight began to grow misty: *caligavit aspectus.* Your inner organs began to quake: *tremuerunt viscera.* Your hands began to fall under their own weight: *brachia conciderunt.* Your trembling tongue came to a stop and barely managed to pronounce the words it was hoping to articulate: *lingua haesit.* Then you were seen approaching the altar to which you were being taken to sacrifice to the idols, trembling and downcast, as though you were being taken there to be sacrified yourselves: *ara illa quo moriturus accessit, rogus illi fuit.*

*

Earth confiscated by a territory of the earth. (Imperial, religious.)

Earth lost in the 'unary', 'human', 'divine' world that no longer recognizes itself as Earth.

Nature in which the sown no longer recognizes the seed.

Being in which the origin is lost.

*

Jean-Baptiste Massillon:[†] If the father no longer finds his resemblance in his son, where is the father? And if the son does not suffer abandonment, where is the father whom the abandoned one calls on in heaven? If we do not embrace abandonment and anguish, passion and the night of agony, then we are but faithless images, are but poorly hewn, discarded stones that can no longer form part of the building and that fit in nowhere.

CHAPTER 5

Nordstrand

Antoine Arnauld and Pierre Nicole hid themselves away in the Ardennes.[†] They said they were two moles trying to advance unseen beneath the surface of this world.

Voltaire said of Arnauld that the pleasure of writing in freedom had been all he ever wanted.

The abbey of Port-Royal conceived the project of buying an island in America and setting up there as the persecuted Puritans had recently done.

They opted in the end for the island of Nordstrand off the coast of Holstein.

*

I look for the name Nordstrand on a map. I look for the coasts of Holstein. Suddenly I realize it is not unusual that I shouldn't find them in atmospheric air. Where is what is lost? Where what was lost is lost, there lies the *last kingdom*. I asked the embankment of the Loire for a share of its shade. Then I discovered it. Then it received me.

*

Rancé wrote to Retz in 1673: Everything is passing away at a fearful rate.[†]

Rancé's other saying: 'Time is lost.'

Human time as the Kingdom where the Lost reigns. Its traces are disappearing at a fearful rate that takes us all with it. *As it disappears, this speed is bringing everything down.* In the chaos of religious and civil wars, it seems everyone thinks only of his childhood, which fades away as he does.

Men and women quickly forget genital joys to reproduce the fears surrounding the decidedly vague sense of expectancy of the as-yet-unsemantized time of their childhoods, which are so long.

As old men they repeat that childhood, to the point of folding back into it. They turn over the straw, their minds rambling. They love it to the point of dying there.

*

We are living in 1571. A Saint Bartholomew's Day atmosphere hangs over France's *banlieues*. The wars of religion are beginning afresh. Democracy is a fierce Protestant religion. Islam is a fearsome sexual religion. There have never been so many myths as there are now, never such competition between myths during human history: Woman deified, Death adored, Democracy more violent and inegalitarian than in the time of Pericles. War of the subject against himself in neurosis, which is merely the secret narrative of subjection. A technicist fetishism. An unplanned, herd-like Cult of Youth. Worse than unplanned—wild, psychotic.

*

No one jumps over his shadow.

No one jumps over his source.

No one jumps over his mother's vulva.

*

Who does not love what he has loved? We must love the lost, and love even the Erstwhile in that which is lost.

Love even the garden in the extinction of nature and even the Paradise in the Garden.

We must love lack and not try to free ourselves from it.

We must love sexual difference;

Love nudity in the orifices of nudity, love loss.

We must adore time.

*

We must renounce the idea of liberty so as still to disobey. We must renounce the idea of liberty so as still to be able to free ourselves. We must detest the now, detest what clings on in the now, what seeks to maintain reality and the tensing of the forces that secure it. We must hate what prevents all access to the unpredictable and the irreversible. We must love the irreversible. We must hollow out the gap between the event and language.

One should never leave behind the Erstwhile, the body or its joy, sin, genitality, silence, shame, anecdotes, the 'Once upon a time', the private, the incomprehensible, the incomplete, the whim, the enigma, the humblest of trivial occurrences, the most ridiculous rumour going back to earliest childhood.

*

Whereas in the life that preceded daylight we were merely a passionate sense of hearing, we become, through birth, producers of sound.

Once we forsake sounds, once we neglect the injunction and the ear, once we break down everything *into letters*, we disobey.

Emerging into the light, choking in the air, we can raise our eyelids and see, we can lower our eyelids and interrupt our sight, we can breathe, we can expel through our mouths the language our mothers' mouths imperceptibly put into them.

*

I prefer the word 'intrusion' to 'exception' because the word *intrusus* is closer to birth. I don't believe art can ever be negative. It knows nothing of negation because it knows nothing of time. Before escaping the norm, it moves closer to life. It is not eccentric: it is at the heart of the centre. It is the act, the actness of the act, the exactness of the *tao*. Creation is in no way removed from anything of the world or anything of life.

It is life itself. It is the way itself.

Intro-ire in Latin means go-in. It is to enter into the path of life. It is to be born.

Intrusus is the one who enters forcibly, who introduces himself so violently, without the right to do so, with the result that he is chased away. He is *the one who is not invited*. This is the magnificent, shared definition of the word 'intruder'.

CHAPTER 6

'Stop breathing!'

I wasn't at the photographer's. I was in the X-ray unit in Reykjavik. This is what every society tells its citizens: 'Stop breathing.'

CHAPTER 7

The Nursling

In 395, when they were in the Sainte-Chapelle at Candes, St Brice announced: 'Martin is a drivelling idiot.'[†]

St Martin came up to St Brice. He said to him, 'Away with you! Away with you! My ears are too close to your mouth for you to speak.'

Despite this, after the death of Martin, Brice was elected bishop by the community of Tours.

*

Many years after St Brice had become bishop, a nun from the Touraine, who happened to be a laundress in his monastery, brought a son into the world and named St Brice as the father. The people of the city of Tours gathered, muttering and grumbling. Taking up stones, they threw them at St Brice. They shouted: 'You are lecherous. You have defiled a *soeur lavandière*. We cannot kiss a finger that is tainted. Give back your ring.'

Brice answered them simply: 'Bring me the child.' The child, who was only thirty days old, was brought to him. He was half asleep in the arms of his mother. He did not cry. St Brice had both of them brought into the apse, beneath the vaulted roof of the church. The bishop of Tours leaned over to the nursling and asked him, in everyone's presence, 'Was it I who begat you?' The baby opened its eyes wide, but made no reply. St Brice put his question in Latin: '*Si ego te genui?*' The thirty-day-old child then answered immediately: '*Non tu es pater meus*' (You are not my father).

The people then asked the child who his father was. But the child said, still in Latin, that even if he remembered the face of the man who had mounted his mother at the moment of his conception, how would he know his name? He also said: 'It wasn't exactly his name that my father was murmuring in the ear of my mother at that point.' In short, the only assurance the nursling could give was that that man was not St Brice. Now, the people, unhappy at the answer they had received from the nursling, still wanted to throw stones.

A decision was taken to proceed to an ordeal, to disarm everyone's anger.

The smith put burning coals in the bishop's hands.

The crowd called on Brice to carry the glowing embers to the tomb of St Martin.

Brice crossed the Loire.

Everyone followed him, murmuring. After he had put the burning brands down on Martin's tombstone, the palms that had held them were unharmed.

*

The crowd then turned around against the nursling's mother.

The sister laundress' breasts were bared and a young man cut them off.

This being done, the woman's body was covered not only with blood, but with milk, because she was still suckling her thirty-day-old child. The nun was stoned by the people of Tours for her lying.

CHAPTER 8

Rome was far off. It was becoming more distant. Once it had been a mistress. Now it had become a memory. From being a memory, it became a phantom. The very idea of a centre for the space of the earth had become something akin to the animals leaping about in the visions of Queen Basina.

The last king of the Romans has a name.

A pontiff, also from Tours, devoted sixteen lines to him that have kept his memory alive.[†]

He was called Syagrius. He was the son of Aegidius. He did not bear the title *magister militum*, nor those of *dux* or patrician that his father had borne. In the late 470s, these mandates had been revoked.

He was simply called *rex Romanorum*, King of the Romans.

The seat of the last kingdom of the last king of the Romans was Soissons. Clovis marched against him with the support of the men of Ragnacaire.[†]

Soissons was the busiest, most populous city of Belgian Gaul. From the top of the hill it looked down over the river Aisne, a wooden landing stage, a great marble porch at the entry to the water and sixty boats.

The private buildings at Soissons were vast, opulent, secretive, marvellous.

The military workshops making breastplates and balistas had aquired a renown that extended beyond the frontier bounding the empire.

It was to the north of the town that the alabaster castle that was the last king's residence lay. Apart from Sofiius, his secretary, the keeper of his library, he was surrounded by a court of cithara players, crows, women for his enjoyment, captains, talking blackbirds, astrologers, fantastical books, amphoras, barking dogs, oak trees. Every day in the sanctuary of the palace, Syagrius hid from the eyes of his circle to sacrifice to the forbidden gods. We are not speaking here of the martyr cobblers of Soissons,[†] but of his silent reading of the exploits of Aeneas from an Egyptian papyrus roll.

*

In 451, Attila had spared Soissons.[†]

In 486, Chlodovecchus, King of Tournai, sent a challenge to Syagrius, last king of the Romans, in the form of a naked girl soiled by her own menstrual blood, the intention being to bring him ill fortune.

Syagrius brought his army before Soissons, between Juvigny and Montécouvé.

King Chararic climbed to the crest of the hill and watched in the company of his warriors, having sworn on the intactness of his head of hair that he would seal a pact of friendship with the victorious party.

The Frankish forces were victorious.

Chararic then gave his support to Clovis.

Syagrius took flight on horseback and sought refuge with Alaric, King of the Visigoths, then ruler of Toulouse. Alaric, fearful of incurring the wrath of the King of Tournai, contravened established custom and surrendered his guest to him. He bound the last king of the Romans hand and foot like a trophy of the hunt and put him in a cart that left Toulouse at dusk and crossed the Gothic frontier in darkest night.

This was how the last king of the Romans was delivered to the Franks.

*

King Chlodovecchus—that is to say, Clovis—took his sword, scraped all the hair from the head of Syagrius—that is to say, from the last king of the Romans—who bled, and clapped him in irons in a limestone cave in the Loire valley. Clovis waited for all to swear their allegiance to him, then secretly had the king beheaded with a single blow. The hair, which had grown back, was about an inch in length and, as it had no curls, King Chlodovecchus could not hold up the head by the top of the skull to present it to his people.

Clovis declared that he was wreaking vengeance on the last king of the Romans for the death of his ancestors, the Frankish kings: a hundred and seventy years earlier, they had been devoured by bears in the amphitheatre.

As the sword of the first king of the Franks approached and he shrank back into the shadows of his cell, Syagrius asked where were the Elysian fields and the gods that protected them.

Clovis made Soissons his royal capital. It was during this campaign that Clovis took all the vases from the churches.[†]

*

Beauty may have an impoverishing effect. The legend that has come down to us through history is at variance with Gregory's chronicle. The text of the man of Tours is as follows: '*Quem Chlodovecchus receptum custodiae mancipari praecepit, regnoque ejus accepto, eum gladio clam feriri mandavit. Quaesivit cum moriebatur ubi essent umbrae.*' Literally: As soon as Clovis had received [Syagrius] from the hands of

[Alaric], he gave the order that he be put under guard. Then, after he had taken possession of his kingdom, he commanded that his throat be secretly cut. As he was expiring, he asked where were the shades, the shadows.

*

It is not known what the last king of the Romans meant by his dying words.

Quaesivit cum moriebatur ubi essent umbrae .

He asked, as he died :

'Where are the shadows?'

*

Did he mean by this—as legend has it—the 'shades', the souls in Hell? Was he trying to refer, with due propriety, to the gods of Olympus, shrouded by the cloud in which they travel? Was he speaking of Aegidius, his father? Of the forces of the Gauls, whose leader he was? Of the bonds that had been formed, in the days of his father, by King Childeric or his wife Queen Basina? Or in the days of his grandfather, King Meroveus? Why had the son of Childeric not respected the oath he had made to the son of Aegidius? Where were the shades (*umbrae*) to bear witness to the pledge that had been given? And seeing that pledge broken and the alliance overthrown, should they not at the moment of this murder in the shadows have been moved to cry out in the forests or the temples, to raise mighty winds and call down curses?

*

The legend that has come down to us lacks plausibility.

The shades invoked by Syagrius are not those of the Christian hell. The dying Syagrius was not Dante at Ravenna.

'He asked where are the shades' means, rather: Come to me, forefathers who respect the pledge given. You fought side by side at the battle of Orleans. Hold still these fingers that are vainly trying

to grasp the hair they have shorn and stay this blade
that is against my throat.

*

Alternatively, the question 'Where are the shades?'
could have meant: Come, Furies, avenge the murder
committed in the shadows. Bring doom upon the
children of the grandson of Meroveus, and let it be
so from generation to generation!

*

'Quaesivit cum moriebatur ubi essent umbrae.' The
king asked: Where are the yellow wasps when the
snow falls on the icy path? Where is Hell? What was
my father looking upon when he let out a little cry
and conceived me? Where is Virgil?

CHAPTER 9

The Ewer

A terrible hand has suddenly intervened upon the earth: the hand of a single form of exchange that has no other purpose than its grasp, no other means than the pressure it exerts, no other rhythm than the monotony of its growth. That hand has imposed its harmony, the concord of a despotic indulgence. It has the fresh, green sound of a crackling, crunching dollar—a sound striving to drown out the voice of languages. For the first time, merchants can address themselves to the entirety of the market they have managed to fashion. This ultimate act of invasion thrills, but also limits them by the unity it imposes. Their interest consists in taking what is produced and selling it to everyone—that is to say, to the human race—at the best price. They foment revolutions in the last empires with the intention of penetrating their frontiers. They draw upon terror to sell peace. At a single moment, they offer up a unique object to the desire of the species, an object whose lifespan seldom outlasts the day of its acquisition. That object is so friable that it is almost an image of itself. It is a gilded ewer taken from a basilica near Soissons, for example—an ewer that is smashed.[†] Woe to him who would not strive to hasten to own this item of wealth, which shines out to everyone, and develop it. Woe to him who has known the invisible and letters, the shadows of the Ancients, silence, the secret life, the useless reign of useless arts, individuality and love, time and pleasures, nature and joy, which are not things that are exchanged at all and which constitute the dark element of the commodity. Every work of art can be defined: it is what electrocutes this light. From the moment it is written, every sentence can be defined: it is what explodes the screen on which the increasingly vague face of a single class of fascinated, viviparous animals shows itself. The destiny of those who use language has not always been hypnosis.

*

'Quaesivit: ubi sunt umbrae?'

The last king of the Romans, descending into the Underworld, asked of it:

'Where is hell?

And where the shades?

Where the banks along the river Acheron and its currentless waters?

Where the Elysian Fields and the caves of Cumae, where Erebus and the pale, translucent souls of the dead?[†]

And the robes full of drained blood, the torches and the three Erinyes?

And Charon's blue bark?

Where is death?

*

This is the second time humanity has verged on unity.

The backcloth of horror against which that unity looms is one humanity has contrived for itself from beginning to end.

Once only a single world exists, there is no way to distinguish between world war and civil war.

The Second World War, in the heart of the preceding century, has forever dissolved the idea of a humaneness within humanity.

The future concerns the earth's crust and the life that had covered it, from the depths of the oceans to the peaks of the mountains.

The past, tombs, memory, stories, ancient languages, the books written in days gone by, the religious, political, artistic and individual traditions that were abandoned, torn away from the legendary spirit that had brought them into being, one after the other, are forever disconnected from the real. We even speak of the languages that no longer have mouths to speak them as dead languages. Yet they are treasures of accumulated joy. In accumulating, that joy becomes concentrated. The meaning, the surprise have not fled them. The future that is to come should not simply *come*, but should *surprise*. The shadows are engulfed in it. 'Where are the shadows if I am no longer?' the last king of the world asked himself after he had left the alabaster castle looking down over the Aisne. It is shadows we must range against images.

CHAPTER 10

'Te loquor absentem.'[†]

'You I address, though you are absent.'

It is you, and you alone, that my voice names behind everything I refer to.

No night comes up without you.

No day rises.

It was said of Hiero of Syracuse that all he lacked to be king,

was the kingdom.

CHAPTER 11

Cras

Zenchiku wrote: That which escapes forgetting is the past in person.[†]

The 'other time' is the *primum tempus* at the time of its recurrence.

The past is built up in each wave of time that advances. The past available to contemporaries is not even the same each time it comes up from the realm of shadow. Mallarmé's past isn't Michelet's and Rembrandt's isn't Vermeer's. Chuang-Tzu's isn't Heraclitus', nor Cervantes' that of Shakespeare.

Nor Emily Bronte's that of Charlotte.

The past lives as nervously and unpredictably as the present into which it protrudes its face.

The past is full of tics, but also crammed with wishes in the shadows.

It is the whole of time that is, on each occasion, transformed by the bark, the hauler, the path beside the bank, the horses of time and their capering, by the weather and hunger.

Time is the freeplay that is left, in the heart of the present situation, between the gradients and velocities, spurtings and outpourings of the past. Menelaus angrily told Agamemnon:

'You don't know what you want: today, yesterday, tomorrow, always something else.'

Irresoluteness is a more profound possibility than freedom, chance a more ingenious disposition than tactics; forgetting, anger, greedy hope and a lying-in-wait followed by a sudden pouncing are effects not of being, but of time.

Every work of art is comparable to a section of rock crashing down into the water; and so is each season. Circles spread out from that crash; they become lost in the future which repeats itself in them, and in the past which they invent. They are lost, but they have not disappeared.

They have not disappeared when already another stone falls the way the earth itself, in time past, was a stone that fell into space,

lived there little by little amid light and water, flowers, birds and dreams, language and death,

and will disappear there.

CHAPTER 12

In the valley in front of the hotel there were horses lying in a field, their heads raised, neither awake nor asleep, like wild beasts whose hunger has left them, like wild beasts whose wildness has forsaken them, like memories of great wild beasts surrounded by barbed wire. One of them snorted as I approached, rose unsteadily on the grass and came towards me with astonishing clumsiness and want of balance and yet stupefying elegance also, as though it were awakening from some thousand-year slumber.

Epicurus wrote: Everyone leaves life as though he had scarcely been born.

CHAPTER 13

The Bark

The fluid, golden light poured from deep in the sky on to the Yonne.[†]

In front of me, on the river in the darkness, the light-bedecked outline of a flat, empty boat, of a boat that seemed empty, was moving quite quickly, going silently downriver.

'Am I disturbing you?'

He was there in front of me, keeping tight to the river bank with the aid of his yellow oar.

'Give me the chain,' I said.

He passed it over.

I tied it to the ramshackle little wooden landing stage in front of my hermitage.

My friend stepped on to the bank.

'You seemed so absorbed . . . '

'I was waiting for you.'

'No, you weren't waiting for me. You were clearly thinking about something else . . .'

'I was gliding along the river.'

CHAPTER 14

As the black clouds in the sky were rent apart, the blue dome of the heavens emerged suddenly in a state of nudity I find difficult to convey in words. It was a fresh, gleaming blue, deep in the dark sky.

CHAPTER 15

Shadows

In 1933, Tanizaki published a short text in which he expressed regret at the loss of shadows and darkness.[†] I think these pages are among the finest ever written in any of the various societies that have arisen over time—societies which the different natural languages have divided up within the general history of the world. His regret was all the more poignant for being provocatively argued. In that argument Tanizaki expressed his nostalgia for the lavatories of old Japan that were places of near darkness, places no longer tolerated by the whole of Japanese society, which had suddenly been won over by a general desire to excrete in dazzling, puritanical, imperialist, American neon light, and to do so into a spotless porcelain pan, surrounded by gleaming white, hygienic tiling and the fake fragrance of flowers.

*

Junichiro Tankizaki expressed regret at the passing of the writing brush, which made less noise than a fountain pen; at the passing

of tarnished metal objects;

of opaque crystal and clouded jade;

of streaks of soot on bricks;

of the peeling of paint on wood;

of the marks of weathering;

of broken branches, wrinkles, unravelled hems, heavy breasts;

of bird droppings on a balustrade;

of the silent, inadequate light of a candle to eat by, or the light of a lantern hanging above a wooden door;

of the freer or dulled or vacillating thought that arises in the human head when it buries itself in shadow, the soul moving closer to the boundary of the teeth;

of the deeper, more hesitant voice that accompanies the glow of the cigarette which catches the eye;

of the more persistent taste of what is eaten and the less haunting impression of the shape and colour of dishes as one grows older, food becoming gradually more connected with the darkness of the body with which it merges.

*

In cooking, what is finest is that which is Lost, whose reign never ends. The fate hovering over the prey that has been eaten constitutes its shadow.

One senses that shadow everywhere.

We are surrounded by its death odour, or the odour of its killing, beyond the remains of fish bone or carcass.

*

Junichiro Tankizaki said his hair stood on end when confronted with the sparkle of steel;

nickel;

chrome;

the invention of aluminium;

the excessive, gleaming whiteness of Western paper;

any china or spectacles.

*

He loved the semi-darkness that tea spreads around its warm, liquid world.

And the colours the little rolled leaf releases as filaments in the water, before they blend into it.

And the reddish and, in some respects, autumnal residue that gradually comes to lie at the bottom of the porcelain bowl.

*

He loved hiding places, associated with darkness and with the enormous floating expanse that darkness contributes.

He loved clothes in handsome dark colours, in browns and greys.

He said the density of thought in dim light was extraordinarily close to the intensity of excitation in embarrassment.

Embarrassment both invades

And vanishes, leaving the mind and

invading

the body, which it tenses.

*

He regretted the passing of art also, meaning by that the original bond art had formed with craft manufacture or, in other words, with the uniqueness of the objects it adds to the world.

He loved dark bowls.

He loved walls of sand.

*

He loved the paucity of light on the body of a woman who removes the linen enveloping her smooth stomach and her naked breasts only to entrust them to the half-light. Her fragrance is stronger, her more naked skin is softer; her features, being more ghostly, are the more feminine. She comes from the past; she is not at odds with the darkness of her parted vulva and reminds us that it is the old abode.

*

He did not distinguish shadow from the traces of the past. He regretted the passing of grime on boxes and rust on knives, nails and flat-headed screws.

He missed the moon, too, as the only night-time light in humble dwellings;

undergrowth and the frightening creatures to be found there;

the thrilling shadow roving and fading beneath trousers and robes;

listening to music with the lamps snuffed out.

*

Junichiro Tanizaki's aesthetic position was resolutely anti-naturalistic his whole life long. He never yielded an inch on the mendacious character of his conceptions and narratives.

Language is a form of lying.

Pluto was called the King of the Shades.

The writer is language devouring itself within the man devoured by the lying that constitutes his core.

*

There is no liar who doesn't conceal the fact he is lying.

The novelist is the only liar who doesn't conceal the fact he is lying.

*

The secret is the only bond between the individuals —in the social shadow, in the sexual half-light—who seek each other out, since that which claims not to be concealed is mere semblance.

*

In reading, there is an expectancy that does not seek to come to anything. To read is to wander. Reading is errantry.

(Beware of knights errant! Beware of novelists!)

Chrétien de Troyes gave a name to *Those Who Go about Strange Lands Seeking Out Strange Adventures.*

(Beware of knights errant! They are out for adventure; they are drawn to calamity.)

*

Lies and metamorphoses are in endless struggle against the real, against the state of things, against the sale of men, animals and objects, against the commands of language and the tyranny of roles in the functioning of groups. Tanizaki took the view that the individual nocturnal position was at the opposite end of the scale from the solar, national order of the Rising Sun.

*

I must at once add some lists to the lists drawn up by Tanizaki.

The lists of Li Yi-chan and those of Marcus Aurelius, cruder and more shameful.

The lists of Sei Shonagon or Shaftesbury, more refined and puritanical.

The lists of *Memor*, which are those of the shadow projected day after day by life.

CHAPTER 16

List from the Year 2001

The surface of the waters that have been stagnating since the first migrations to the stilted villages in the grey Etruscan lakes.

The pools caused by rain, around whose edges tiny, black-as-ebony frogs suddenly jump.

The great white wave on the Carnac shore at ten.

The sordidness of the shadows in the Paris dustbin when you hastily raise its lid to slip in an empty tuna tin.

The slime trails of snails on leaves or on the dry earth between the flower spikes.

The sugar-sticky, mud-spattered fingers of the little children at Sens.

The sleeve of the worn-out, dark-blue silk jacket.

*

The pile of inexplicably growing dust which the broom pushes before it anywhere at all in the world.

*

The overripe pear, moist with juice, and its broad, thick peelings on the round wooden tray of the high-chair against the wall in the kitchen at Verneuil.[†]

The smell of old dung and of hay on suddenly entering the darkness and coolness of the cowshed at Garet in the Périgord thirty years ago.

A child opening his mouth and wanting to show you a cavity in a milktooth that will be placed, once it has fallen out, in the shade of the mouse hole.[†]

The black hair shed into the horn comb that has been left on the sink shelf by the woman you still desire.

CHAPTER 17

I said to myself, 'I'm going to go see. I'm going to go see what I don't know. My lips will tremble. I shall suffer. Why not?'

*

On the screen, a good image is a face that doesn't cast a shadow.

If a writer were appreciated for showing himself, it would be his body that was in demand, not his lost voice, his stray voice that is almost silent on the page.

Every being who shows himself turns his back on the realm that is not visible.

*

Writing is not a natural way of being of natural language. It is a parlance that has become a stranger to dialogue. It is a strange parlance. It is language become language-to-be. In times past, in the first neolithic empires, writing wrested prehistoric humanity from the worlds of dreams and the imagination. Pregeneric humanity was buried in its picture caves, as in its dreams. Beyond oral, admonitory, hypnotic, mythic language, generic humanity caused *isolated* language to blossom—in the form of letters.

Beginning with the written word, that humanity produced a more lonely parlance, language without context, an inner language, secrecy, an entirely new area of shade.

The dominant morality, resorting once again to the voice in the image, the voice issuing from the image, is once again a world of the deified, despotic dead, treating human beings like children or slaves.

Like sparrows, like skylarks, like bulls: loaves, mirrors, rags.

CHAPTER 18

On the Arrest of Monsieur de Saint-Cyran on 14 May 1638

There is in the thought of Monsieur de Saint-Cyran a conception of inner freedom so intransigent that it would have devastated any society.[†] At least, that is what Richelieu felt immediately when he received him at the Palais du Louvre. He took fright. And that is what induced him to have the man arrested, for no good reason, on 14 May 1638. Theological problems were invoked only after his incarceration. So many doctrinal excuses to conceal an intuition that had initially taken the form of mere fear.

Saint-Cyran cast such an absolute gaze on the century that he seemed to condemn any worldly activity.

He denied the legitimacy of family ties in God.

He inveighed against professional activities.

He scorned political duties.

He denied all bonds that were merely human, merely collective, merely universal.

He preached a way of life in which one turned one's back on the world with radical violence.

He violently advanced the proposition, paradoxical outside the walls of Port-Royal des Champs, of a Society of Solitaries.

The man became a distant 'gentleman' who addressed others formally as a means of fleeing from them. Just before withdrawing forever into *lectio divina*.

Monsieur de Pontchâteau had made the Granges de Port-Royal des Champs his hermitage.

Monsieur de Pontchâteau had at first collected miniatures, before he became infatuated with books. From the moment he began to enjoy reading them, he lived for them alone. He was always ready with this phrase from *The Imitation of Christ*:[†]

> *In omnibus requiem quaesivi et nusquam inveni nisi in angulo cum libro* (I have sought rest throughout the whole world and found it nowhere, except in a corner with a book).

*

To live in the corner—*in angulo*—of the world.

*

In the *angle mort*—the blind spot—where the visible is no longer visible to sight.

In the dead zone where the two human rhythms (first the cardiac, then the pulmonary) embrace and around which they generate sonic ecstasy and, perhaps, music—and, from music, time.

*

Such is Lake Avernus and such the gates and the howling that are beneath Tartarus.[†]

Such are the lakes the ancient Etruscans made for, carrying the severed, re-modelled heads of their ancestors on spears.

Such were the boiling pitch and Cerberus:[†] the visible does battle with the invisible. But only the visible shines. Only its victory shines, since even its defeat is brilliant.

*

One must meditate on this point: the victory of the invisible does not shine.

*

One day in April 30 CE, Jesus was taken from the house of Caiaphas to the Praetorium. It was morning. The sun was rising. Governor Pilate came into the Praetorium and asked Jesus:

> Thine own nation and the chief priests have delivered thee unto me: what hast thou done?[†]

Jesus replied:

> '*Regnum meum non est de hoc mundo*' (My kingdom is not of this world).[†]

*

The living are not shades. They are perhaps dead people swathed in clothes and shining.

They genuflect now—with gleaming pairs of eyes and all dressed alike—before the same screens, with the same desire.

Demagogic, egalitarian, fraternal—these words indicate the same attitude: murderers watching each other out of the corner of their eyes. They share in the same aversion to all forms of superiority. They huddle against one another, clinging to their anxiety as though it were a sex organ about to be taken from them, begging for an additional form of protection, a further taboo, shackle or medical drug.

This terror in the face of independence and desire turns naturally into hatred against those who call for a little shade, with the aim of hiding their pleasures from everyone's sight.

For them, freedom is an outbreak of disorder.

They are afraid if they are not asleep.

*

At the dawn of the last century, Walter Benjamin wrote that the inventions of photography and cinematography had introduced—into the very heart of the things they had brought to light—*the absence of shadow*.

*

Two arts wiped out the living aura of the play of light and shade within nature.

Alongside the technique of lighting and in addition to the expression 'taking' a photo, photographers used the term 'definition' to refer to the sharpness of outline of the entities in their 'negatives'.

A taking, a predation which snatched away the veil of shadow that lay upon flesh in the eyes of all those who imagined it.

And reduced the blur of distance surrounding flesh as it bared itself.

A shadow calculated, more or less, by the body preparing itself for love, as it stripped itself, discreetly or embarrassedly, before opening its heart in the shadows of its joy.

*

One cannot offer a visible counterweight to the universal domination of light without it contributing itself to light's reign.

One cannot set a containing wall or a dyke against it without its expansive power immediately breaching them.

That ocean knows no shores.

Everything is immersed in it.

Fish that still rise to the surface. A gulp to stave off death.

That gulp: reading.

*

Pluto is the god of the other world.

He is *The one who sees in the shadows*.

Shakespeare wrote: Pluto winks while Orpheus plays.

Ploutos in ancient Greece referred to fortunes that shine in the night, fortunes in silver and gold.

Ploutôn was the god dealing in treasures-buried-under-the-earth.

Plutarch—*ploutarchos*—in Greek meant the master of buried riches.

*

Latin *vulgus* translates the Greek word *demos*.

Vulgarity is our soul: we speak the language of the people, the *langue vulgaire*. Our breath (*psyche*) throws back the echo of the language of the group (*vulgus*).

Our inner, familial, linguistic lives are increasingly homogeneous, civilized, collective: heterogeneity is not man's destiny.

Cultural, historical homogeneity—such is man's destiny.

Natural, original heterogeneity—such is the destiny of art.

Fragmentation is the soul of art.

The equal, interchangeable human beings of democratic regimes had their counterparts in the unpredictable individualities of the worlds of romance. The *littera* stood over against the *stips*; the *individuum* over against the *vulgus*; aristocratic *otium* over against democratic *negotium*.

*

There is a world in which ages are not equal, the sexes not undifferentiated, roles not equivalent and civilizations not easily confused with one another.

There is a world in which the ignorant are not the equal of the learned, the oral does not have the same 'voice' as the written, nor the *vulgus* as the *atomos*, nor barbarians as civilized beings.

There is another world.

*

There is a world that belongs to the shore of the Lethe.

That shore is memory.

It is the world of novels and sonatas, the world of the pleasure of naked bodies that love the half-closed blind or the world of the dream that loves it even more closed, to the point where it feigns the darkness of night or contrives it.

It is the world of magpies on graves.

It is the world of solitude required for reading books or listening to music.

The world of tepid silence and idle semi-darkness where thought drifts, then suddenly seethes with excitement.

*

Where flesh stands erect or parts.

We are viviparous creatures. We lived before we were born. It so happens that our hearts beat before we drew breath. Our ears heard before our lips discovered the existence of the air. We swam in dark water before our eyelids were open, before our eyes were dazzled, then blinded, then saw; before our throats dried, then choked for a moment, then came to eat air and to imitate words whose *intonation* seemed reassuring.

*

God pushed away the amphora containing the thick, dark wine.

He got up suddenly from the table, laid down his outer garments, unfolded a towel, which he wrapped around his thighs, took an ewer, poured water into a basin, sank to his knees, washed the ankles, washed the feet, washed the toes of the young men around him, and washed the toenails of each of his disciples.

He wiped their toes and said:

'*Si de mundo fuissetis mundus quod suum erat diligeret. Quia vero de mundo non estis propterea odit vos mundus*' (If ye were of the world, the world would love his own: but because ye are not of the world, therefore the world hateth you).[†]

Then he turned to Peter, who was protesting his love and loyalty, and with some irritation told him that he who claimed to be his friend would deny his existence three times before the cock crowed to mark the rising of the sun in the next day's sky.

*

They had razed the houses they had inherited from their fathers.

They no longer built tombs for them.

The treasures they had intended to pass on for their sons' delight they stowed in attics and cellars, behind the railings of stately homes, in museums and in bank strongboxes and, since they had stopped seeing the beauty of these things, they ceased then to be intelligible. Even rhetoric, at the margins of language, which enables us to loosen the tie that strangles everyone's soul with the use of group-speak, was thrown on the scrapheap. Even death—in the form of the rite surrounding it, which lightened the burden of family ties—we have thrown aside like detritus from another age, whose presence unsettles us and whose formal decomposition and smell must no longer be inflicted. Nature itself—the wild beasts of old, the raptors, the forests, the monsters—we have either massacred or diverted into domestication on our farms or heroic roles in our zoos. The old exigencies with their names, the prodigious delights with their corresponding forms of modesty, the proud designs with their achievements, the terrible fears with their songs have all begun to lose their names that once were on our lips. As time advanced, and waste and rubble with it, as palaces crumbled and men and their cities covered the earth with charnel houses and flattened the ruins, disappearance itself disappeared. The tyranny of the absence of complex human language was now exerted, raising no obstacle to fascination with the light. Images, artificial dependencies, universal clothing and industrial objects became idols coveted by all.

The few who make the difference between the majority and the totality (prevented from forearming themselves by their weakness and division) have been crushed.

Beauty, freedom, thought, written human language, music, solitude, the second kingdom, deferred pleasures, tales, love's preliminaries, contemplation and clear-sightedness are mere angles, corners; they are merely different names for a single thing, a single enfolding of subject, reality and language. These names matter little. Their memory has been wiped out so completely that those born since their disappearance do not even feel any painful yearning for them.

*

As the world grew old, it receded into the past. As the past receded, its loss seemed the more irremediable.

The more irremediable that loss seemed, the more inconsolable was the abandoned soul who retained the uncertain memory of it in his heart. As the loss compounded the sense of abandonment, nostalgia grew greater. The greater the nostalgia grew, the heavier was the anxiety. The heavier that anxiety became in the heart, the more the throat tightened. The more the throat tightened, the more the voice was wound up to the highest pitch, and this is the first dawn and the first sun.

CHAPTER 20

I had put my shirt out to dry on the terrace of the old villa at Mogador. It was white. The mist surrounded it, prolonging its whiteness against the white baluster. I looked out to sea. The mist generated by the sun, which was already rising, was invading the Punic port.

On the left, the *medina* had disappeared into the mist.

There came an invasion of butterflies.

*

The sea was smooth, foamless, glittering, resplendent. Each wave was like a great golden tile rising and moving forward.

CHAPTER 21

The Snuffers

Ancient China and Japan drew on the teachings of
the Indians, but they were not the only ones to do so.
The trading posts of Augustus' and Marcus Aurelius'
ancient empire joyfully received those teachings and
passed them down. The Sceptics also handed them
on. We are speaking here of the kingdom of Josaphat,
son of King Abenner.[†] Josaphat was overcome by
Barlaam. He told him: The universe is a tissue of
images that are illusory. Men riding in chariots, children on all fours, elephants with six tusks, domes and
golden palaces, immense mantles of snow, rubies and
lapides lazuli, three- or five-stringed musical intru-
ments, eighty-four thousand women, the swastika of
the year revolving upon itself. The world is a peacock
wheel. There are no images that do not play their
part in the illusion and its store of amazements, that

do not contribute to reproducing them—and lovingly reproducing themselves in them—endlessly. History is a succession of hasty intrigues screaming out an endless repetition. One can keep a list of the murders: to do so is known as making a chronology of kings. Space being this chain of stereotyped images, time being this concatenation of sempiternal causes, he who has not poured out his past is condemned to relive it. The real is never an image of reality. The real is enigma. The Sanskrit word for enigma is *brahman*. It is an eternal, prodigiously active present. It has two features: it is incomprehensible and it is hallucinatory. I would venture to suggest that the German word *ersatz* translates the Sanskrit *brahman*. The sleeping soul is a spectator watching an involuntary performance. When it awakes, the mind of the sleeper, as he opens his eyes, discovers an empty mirror. There are no gods. Belief is a mammalian dream. Politics, producing a family, social life and metaphysical thinking are also theatrical performances, in which the soul dreams that it plays a role, in which it dreams that it will brandish its spear, that it is stamping its heel on the floor, that its eyes are delivering flashes of lightning.

Individua can hope only to tend towards the state of wakefulness.

The word *buddha* is a common noun meaning, simply, the awakened.

But waking is such an unpleasant thing for those whose desire rises up in sleep on the occasion of a dream.

A wife who cannot have children handles the dolls that are for sale on the stall tenderly.

*

Fragments do not exist in nature. The tiniest of pieces is still the totality. Every crumb is the universe and this latter is a tiny hair lost in the tresses of the doll that the hand of the barren woman is caressing on one of the street-sellers' stalls.

All is lost.

Everything is as lost as a drop of water in the immense expanse of the sea.

What is the sea?

Each ocean is a tear of time.

Who weeps in the depths of Being?

*

Each time, the sea advances.

Each time, it retreats.

With each wave, it advances its *golden tile*.

With each fall, it draws back the curved pocket of its shadow.

Between hallucination and disorder, the real breathes like a child playing: a jolt as capricious in effect as it is imaginary in perception. Within the real that breathes, time is as unintelligible as the world is phantasmic. The warp and woof of generations and metamorphoses produce the same impatient, inexplicable picture. And so the whimsically playing child is just as much a garrulous old man rambling on. It is a repetition, in the same way that cats have sat watching since time began.

It was always what we knew by heart that caught us off guard.

A verse in the Vedas reads: I am an echo standing before a mirror.

There is no way of not being surprised by echoes of images (by reproductions of flesh due to mothers), by reflections of sounds (by scraps of old forenames already employed in the language of fathers).

*

The body, sexual difference, death and affection are reflections, like daffodils or carp, like the word *brahman*, like square circles. Just as the different sexes suddenly lock together with a shudder, and just as the elements of things are assembled, so souls are transported. They transmigrate from mothers to daughters, from grubs or caterpillars to butterflies and cockchafers, from singers to drums, from murderers to lutes and viols. This is a continuous streaming. It is what makes it possible to interpret the uninterpretable.

Tukaram has a phrase that captures this: I have suffered alarming ills. I know not what my past still has in store for me.[†]

Plotinus said that successive reincarnations were like a man sleeping in different beds.[†]

All one's dreams, words, acts and intentions weave the body that is to come.

The Sanskrit word *karma* designates this weave, which is this product of acts without consideration of their meaning.

*

Acts burn. Sexes burn. All is on fire, all is desire. All is thirst for the *ersatz* and for the death that is the attractant force within it. All is servility and sleep. The consciousness of human beings may be compared to the flame of a lamp lit in the night. That flame can be snuffed out.

The Sanskrit word *nirvana* refers to those two-pronged snuffers used for extinguishing the wick of a candle or for preventing it from smoking.

We have here the dream that knows no one is dreaming it.

Between images and nothingness there is a precipice. There is only one passageway by which to cross it. Silent Sir Lancelot advances along the 'Sword Bridge'. It is so perilous that few take up the challenge and none can say if anyone has ever crossed it (since no dreamer is behind this dream or, in other words, since no god guards the bridge swaying above the abyss).

He doffs his gloves and grasps it, bare as it is.

This is art.

CHAPTER 22

Once the flame is nipped between the fingers, darkness is immediately spread around.

Just as darkness surrounded the bare limbs and shaven head of Syagrius in the shadows of the gaol that lay below the embankment of the Loire.

The last king of Rome asked (*quaesivit*), as he was dying (*cum moriebatur*): Where? (*ubi*).

Where was the *where* from which the world emerged?

Where the *where* into which it disappeared?

He asked, as he was dying, where the prongs of the snuffers were. Where was extinction? And where dreamless sleep?

Where is the mirror on which the reflection does not settle?

CHAPTER 23

Where are we? At the centre of the dawn.

When do we live? We are born in the birth of the star above the earth.

The Inuit myths all explain the settling of men (in Inuit, the word *inuit* means men) in the region of dawn.

The first sign in all the stories was the constellation of events marking the arrival of spring (salmon running back upstream, reproduction, renewal).

There is only one hero whose return is awaited in the stories of men, and that is spring.

And that is why spring is the age of heroes.

But the *investigium* at the heart of the investigation is the dawn.

This is a very strange thing to conceive. It is always the reborn sun. What is sought in the search is the first age, the *primum tempus*, the *printemps*, the spring. At the origin of societies, what was sought in the nomadic quest was the force of time, the initial time of time, the powerful time of time, the return of the living, of the growing, of the nascent, after the hunger, after the impoverishment of the gifts of nature, after the deaths of the winter.

Where human time is concerned, the content of the past *is* the new, is renewal, is the source, is life gushing back. The word *new* posed a problem in ancient Rome: it indicated the non-past, that which did not preserve custom. The Romans were the ancient people who meditated longest on the theme of the new, as we can see from the emperor Claudius' very strange statement: 'The oldest things have been extremely new.'

Novissima. The very newest things are the originals.

(The most ancient things were once the newest of things).

*

At dawn, there is no differentiation between the imaginary and reality.

They are both *ante saecula*.[†]

At dawn, there is perpetual madness and perpetual terror. (Perhaps it is the same with animals. This would explain why wild animals are so easily startled).

*

Time derived from the period of predators watching and then leaping on their prey.

The ancestor of time lived concealed in the two phases of the first *dance-to-the-death*.

The basis of time is the *qui-vive*.

Being on the *qui-vive*.

Remaining perpetually on the *qui-vive*.

The temporal tension of prehuman life in the pure state.

The *qui-vive* is experience in the original state.

It is the life of prey, the *qui-vive*. It is the life of prey in the foreconsciousness of predation and the foreconsciousness of death.

CHAPTER 24

I know the daybreak well. I've never missed it. Even in planes, I open the little plastic shutter that the hostess has ordered us to close, so as to spy out. At whatever time it might be in the circular, celestial staggering of the hours, I know the time of day's first gleam.

Behind the morning's gleam stands the uncertain threshold of the earth.

Daybreak is to the day what spring is to the year, that is to say, what the baby is to the dead man.

*

Daybreak drags a swirl of mist over rivers and lakes. It's a veil that interposes itself between the rising sun and its reflection which spreads into the surrounding region of air. It is its own heat that makes it impossible to see it at the moment of its birth. We never know that which is beginning at its actual commencement. With us, every cause is a recapitulated, fictional one.

We never know what is ending at the moment of its true end. Every farewell is a word we hope to see as a conclusion. Yet it begins nothing and ends nothing.

CHAPTER 25

In August 1999, I unloaded six cases of Epineuil on the banks of the Yonne and two grey jute mailbags filled with books. I dragged them on to the lawn.

That was a good start to the summer. I had to hope I would see no one.

Not a man. Not a child. Not even the wasps.

Not even the enormous, frantic beetles when you're reading on the sun-lounger that's been pulled on to the lawn or dragged further off into the chubby, white flowers of the clover patch.

Not even the field mice pitter-pattering in the dust of the dry attic floorboards as you're falling asleep.

Not even the female mosquitoes that bite you suddenly while you are dreaming.

Not even, within your dreams—and worse than female mosquitoes—memory.

Not even language itself.

There wasn't a plane in the sky.

Not the slightest sound of a transistor radio wafting over.

Not a hint of a tractor engine.

Not a lawnmower.

Not a cock treading a hen.

Not a dog.

Not a local disco.

Not the slightest affectation of cheerfulness around me that might make me want to kill myself forthwith. Happiness welled up inside. I read. I was engulfed by happiness. I read all summer long. Happiness engulfed me all summer long.

CHAPTER 26

The Immortal King of the Ages

If something came from nothing, we'd constantly be seeing terrifying creatures rising out of the seas or skies—screaming women, dumb warriors, tanks, dragons, birds, snakes. We do see them. We suddenly saw planes bursting out of the sky and heading towards towers, towards symbols, towards treasures.

*

The most harmful temptation known to man isn't evil. Or money. Or the stupefying pleasures and diverse ecstasies it brings in its wake. Or power and all the perversions to which it leads. Or sublimation and all the imaginary sentiments to which it gives rise. It is death.

*

Massillon: Remember that temporal rewards are not worthy of those who serve *the immortal king of the ages*. Remember it is good fortune to lose what we are not permitted to love.

The immortal king of the ages is death.

*

Humanity invented death around 100,000 BCE.

Death as invention, if not as drive (it was Sabina Spielrein who invented the expression 'death drive' in Vienna at a Wednesday meeting).[†]

Explosion of death in the blue sky, visible to the naked eye, on Tuesday, 11 September 2001, above the city of New York.

The predator dies, the prey dies, predation dies—everything dies in the moment of its seeing.

*

In hac flamma.[†]

Upsurge of death visible to the naked eye, like the 'Little Boy' mushroom cloud.[†]

View in a moment of time of all the places of the earth.

The last word penned by Freud: *Kriegspanik.* (Curiously translated into French as *atmosphère de guerre.*)

*

Absentia. Abesse. Not to be there. To be missed. *Living* upsurge of death.

Izumi Shikibu: When I see the smoke above the flame, I think, When shall I be seen like that?[†]

Au 'près' de la flamme. Praesentia. Present to the flame.

He who is not present cannot reply.

He who is not close to—*auprès de*—the invention of natural languages cannot reply.

He who is not close to (*prae*) the invention of the question cannot question.

He who does not reply to the inhuman call *at the site*.

CHAPTER 27

Saint Bartholomew's Day

In the arts, there is no such thing as progress. Where the marvellous is concerned, there is no such thing as time. Between stags' antlers and wild beasts on the damp cave walls of Lascaux, the red cherries in the atrium at Stabiae, and the dead hare and hen blackbird depicted in the murals at Herculaneum, where is the increase in beauty?

There is no moral progress. There has been no diminishment of misdeeds if we look at the years constituting the middle of the last century or examine those that closed and opened it. Or those that are opening the coming century. It is an unexampled abyss. It is perhaps the first abyss history has encountered on its path. Abyss is a Greek word meaning *bottomless*. It is the first abyss opened up by the times. There was a time before this abyss. There will perhaps be a *post bellum*, but its definition is the question which, henceforth, visits the time that human languages have constructed. The concept of the abyss, now unprecedented in its vertigiousness, relates not so much to irremissible sin as to endless fear. Given the possibility the earth has found of destroying itself, dread devastates the very idea of that which is nascent within what is supposed to come unpredictably—and always radically—in the future. The natural beauty of the earth is being extinguished as an act of human will. Erotic desire has never known more abrupt retribution. Death, anxiety and lamentation are no longer daily blemishes, but monarchs the more omnipotent for having become pious. Water is given for money. We give a dead man to the earth for money. We give the sun for money. The seas are full of pirates and the skies have welcomed them too. Like the first heavenly bodies, they have become its heroes. Each nation is chosen of the father and produces, as if merely by breathing, a column of refugees. The gods and their horrific retinue are back.

*

The world in which we live represents an exception in the course of History. A tragic exception has caused its decay and, a backwards look has added itself to this exception and led, in turn, to further decay. Two abysses: (1) The German concentration camps leading to the Little Boy bomb. (2) The past in person re-emerging for the first time in history. During the twentieth century, the human past increased at a stroke by hundreds of thousands of years, by thousands of primitive societies never before studied, by an immemorial, continuous Erstwhile, by an entire unexhumed earth.

The vestiges of humanity, thus far invisible to the human eye, began to proliferate.

So much for human *vestiges*.

*

As for the human *visage*, slavery, Christianity, the trenches, gas warfare, the various fascisms, mass deportations, global wars, communist dictatorships and democratic imperialism have finally destroyed its features. There is no longer any hallucinogenic humanity. There is a prodigious, irreversible, sense-less, tempestuous, terrible disorientation.

*

I date the globalization of warfare on the earth's crust from the year 1853. After the genocide of the American Indians and their transportation ('trans-portation' is a word the Germans and the Turks picked up on in the decades that followed), after the genocide of black Africans—democratically flaunted segregation and slavery— the Americans turned their gaze on the rest of the world.

Commodore Matthew Perry triggered the two world wars in the summer of 1853 in the Bay of Edo.

The Japanese shogun, alerted by his men, anxiously observed the American paddle-steamers that dropped anchor in the harbour. The Japanese shogun addressed this message to the American officer:

'We do not wish a devilish humanity to enter our territory. We ask you kindly to return to your country and remain there under the venerable protection of your dead. For, in times gone by we have met the Christians and it was not a happy experience.'

In response, Commodore Perry, at the prow of his ship, shouted over his loud-hailer to the shogun of Edo:

'Either open your borders to free trade or we shall impose it on you by force.'

What Commodore Perry called free trade meant American commerce.

American commerce is quite close to what the ancient Romans called the *Pax*.

No one has ever known what these words (free, peace) meant, either in English or Latin.

The Commodore was flanked by his paddle-steamers and steam corvettes. He slowly tilted his guns and armed them. Then, amid cries of admiration for the four extraordinary ships that were threatening them, the Japanese sailors and fishermen who had gathered on the quayside became targets.

The Americans fired.

The Japanese yielded.

*

The Western world then set about protecting ethnology. Field studies became honourable pretexts for beleaguering those ends of the earth that were still closed to the use of fiduciary money, and for infecting the eyes of the poorest with desire in order to destroy them with a mirage.

Gifts of medicine and food destroyed traditions. Through assistance, freedom became sedentarized. Subjecting human groups to industrial products and alcohol, that assistance opened them up to useless consumption and stupefaction. Having first grabbed them with money, it tied them in to credit and social humiliation.

*

The Inuit have this proverb: Gifts make slaves as whips make dogs.

The Inuit employed this proverb after they had seen the *Amerlaqaat* descend from the sky and invade the kingdom of Thule, without even declaring war on them. This sent them into great transports of panic, as they saw two gigantic military bases inexplicably being built amid their igloos, in the centre of the dawn.

The beauty of a bygone proverb was of no use to them.

The Inuit discovered how three millennia can be wiped away in ten years.

Then they discovered how money is a subtler means of domination than weapons, because it has all the time in the world to menace us in the depths of our souls, with debt as its instrument.

*

The political question is always a single question. The political question is how to foresee the past that lies in wait. The question is never: What future for our children? The question of imminent terror is always imminent. The eternal question is always: What is about to return? If I use the word 'always' here—French *toujours*—it is because I am proposing to deal with that which *is* on the basis of the rending of time. All days, every day. We must *every day* head off the death that fascinates sociality.

*

In the wake of the Saint Bartholomew's Day massacres,[†] humanists and Renaissance thinkers in sixteenth-century France felt immense horror.

That horror of another Saint Bartholomew's Day had consequences. The very first of these was a political revolution. The idea of the French nation was strengthened. Feudalism began to be condemned. Religion became less collective; it became an inward matter. The authority of the state increased and began to impose its anonymous, atheistic constraint.

What added to the stupefying nature of the twentieth century was that nothing political, religious, xenophiliac, national or international came out of the discovery of the concentration and extermination camps Germany had built. Pogroms began again; camps proliferated; ferocity found many other faces; torture techniques were refined; terror grew.

*

It happens that regimes may, at times, be contemptible, institutions dishonourable, beliefs cowardice, solidarity shame, disobedience virtue, and the Erstwhile fierceness and pride.

*

The earth has been turning for 3,500 million years. Humanity has lived for one million years. The history of human civilizations has lasted for 10,000 years, without being either continuous or evolutionary. The civilized, artistic, noetic, literary part is only an imperceptible fraction of the species *Homo*. Imperceptible by the species itself, as a general rule. There have been only a few works, a few objects, a few sounds, a few books, a few walls glimpsed by a few human beings who, from time to time, bow reverentially to them.

*

There was a time—a long time—when men and women left on the earth only excrements, carbon gas, a little water, a few images and their footprints.

*

Over the last 600 million years, the earth has passed through seven mass extinctions of species. The first dates from the beginning of the Cambrian, 540 million years ago. We are contemporaries of the last of these extinctions. By the end of the twenty-first century, half of the plants and animals that still exist will be extinct.

The following will have disappeared:

4,327 species of mammals;

9,672 species of birds;

98, 749 species of molluscs;

401,015 species of coleoptera;

6,224 species of reptiles;

23,007 species of fish.

The Eden is gradually receding from the Garden.

CHAPTER 28

Last Farewell

In the valleys of the Clidame and the Tialle, a particular look was known as the 'last farewell'.

The coffin was set down in silence beside the grave.

The village priest prayed, sprinkled holy water and pronounced the blessing in silence.

In silence, those present moved to the edge of the tomb and simply cast this lengthy farewell gaze.

They did not throw earth or flowers or money, but simply gave this look.

In adjacent, neighbouring valleys—rival, competing valleys—the priest named the dead man, praised his life and chanted. Family, officiating priests and friends threw the pot of incense, the mourning bands, the candle of agony, the gloves, the carrying shafts and a passion cross on to the coffin as it lay in the grave. After bowing to the dead man, they left the cemetery, went back to his house and took the palliasse from the bed. They walked out some way from the village and burned the dead man's palliasse at a crossroads beyond the parish boundary. Burning the dead man's palliasse at a crossroads meant forbidding him to return to his house. How was he to find a bed again? In this way, he was forced on to his last long journey.

But such fears were not felt at all in the valley of the Clidame. Nor was there anything of the sort in the valley of the Tialle. The 'farewell look' sufficed for all purposes. Sufficed for 'leaving'.

CHAPTER 29

Han Yu

Han Yu was born in 768, passed the imperial examination in 792 and loathed Buddhism.[†] He did not bow when a bone of the Buddha's arrived at Chang'an. He expressed his indignation in writing— that is to say, dangerously—against the favour accorded to a bone. He wrote short treatises in severe, concentrated prose. One day, he spread out the five fingers of his hand. He said enigmatically that he still had, between each of his fingers, *the shadow of the first dawn.*

He perfected the so-called ancient prose style (*gu-wen*). Crispness of syntax, precision of diction, repetition of grammatical particles and clarity of statement characterized that style.

He said: The grass that grows grows.

He detested ellipsis, religion, slackness of knots in ropes, slackness in the morals of city dwellers, slackness in the embraces of lovers.

He loved paths in the shade of evening, the dense mist before day fully dawns, gusting wind.

In the poem *Shan shi*, he writes: May I be bound to the shade and to a companion! We should *all three* live to a great age without ever returning.

He was banished twice.

He died.

Buddhism and flabby prose outlived Han Yu.

*

To a nun who asked him if it was useful for her to speak inwardly in her prayers, Monsieur de Saint-Cyran answered, 'No. Human beings are playthings. Our lives are prisons. When language is at our bidding, we erect ruins among the dead leaves and the moss.'

Art is the *tiniest leaf*.

The weakest leaf, since it is the smallest of those that grow.

Always the newest, hence always the smallest.

It is a remnant of nature within culture. It is birth. In each and every thing, birth is an attempt to live again.

Art knows only rebirths. Nature is the origin. Art is never greater than the tiniest of springtimes shooting its sticky whitish buds from the tips of its branches.

*

What in French is called a *contre-feu* consists in setting fire to a wood, which will then burn towards a forest fire, so that a firebreak is established across which the flames cannot leap. It is assumed that this little gap will halt the immense blaze simply by starving it of fuel.

A counterpoint is an additional line of music diverging from the melodic line. To write in counterpoint means to write in response to the main energy of the piece.

A counter-deed is a secret, written agreement that cancels a public contract.

How are we to set up a counterweight to what has become the general economy, to the interests it causes to proliferate, without bringing down immediate persecution or famine upon ourselves?

How to stiffen the spirit of three or four against the authority of everyone?

These three or four hide themselves away. They found fragile secret societies. They are forced to pretend to espouse the jovial ways and aggressive acts of the barbarians. They show themselves in their cities, their temples, their amphitheatres. But in the corners—that is to say, *in angulo*, in the shadows, in secret—they slip each other, not sectarian or promotional pamphlets (as one might slip someone pornographic photos) or national ones (that is to say, banknotes), but works published in nine copies, or memories of books, or photocopies of the old books themselves which, among all the commodities for sale, have nothing to sell whatever.

These grey, photocopied pages—these imageless images—punch holes in time.

*

The market can say, 'This works, that doesn't work.' What more could the market say? And the crowd of spectators at the games, piled on to the terraces, squatting on the steps, their eyes already gleaming at the spectacle of death in preparation, cheer and stamp their feet.

In days gone by, they read, they listened, they touched, they spoke. They didn't say, 'I go along, I buy, I cheer, I stamp my feet.' They said, 'That enlightens me.' Or, 'That moves me.' They had in mind to embellish the world, to make time more fertile, not to promote day-to-day sales in the here and now, in order to hasten obsolescence. To extend their minds further, to feel freer, to speed up the workings of the mind, to make it more independent, more lucid—this was what they liked. Not finding a buyer for some cheap junk or for a *jug from Soissons* one second before they were destroyed.

*

There is now only one empire and the sole mediation running through it isn't even a linguistic meaning any more, but a monetary equivalence.

They put the Vikings in charge of preserving Rome;

they put the Spaniards in charge of preserving the temples of the Aztecs;

the Portuguese in charge of Edo harbour;

the Sun King in charge of a razed Port-Royal.

*

Images are representations of nothing. Without language they are meaningless. What do the scenes depicted on the walls of paleolithic caves mean? We shall never know, for want of the mythic tales they condensed or pre-lettered.

Images are pre-human.

They date from a time before there were natural tongues—natural languages—in human mouths.

I maintain the following: that which dreaming invented in some animals exerts a fascination prior to all meaning.

With the letter now useless, the signifier shorn of a signified, money is the mediating element of the mutually competing desires.

*

Georges Bataille's *The Accursed Share* is one of the finest books of the shadows.[†] Human societies court chance and death. The whole world serves as a basis for the general exchange that is what we once called warfare. The single market has its single goal, which is itself. The market has sought to expand into the totality of available space.

It has succeeded.

The available space has now extended to the earth.

As a result, the earth has entered into competition with itself. Competition, expansion and profit are rational only in the limited, dual state. On a wider scale, the moment the propensity to grow finds nothing to oppose or compete with, it becomes the whirling of a shaman before he collapses ecstatically into the dust which the weight of his body throws up in the moment of his fall.

CHAPTER 30

The Vestals

The Being, since the origin, of everything that is abolishes any questioning by satisfying that questioning in essence. Language says, 'It is . . .' Before any question, it has always already replied.

The quest must be without object (without religion, without being, without response).

Even language must not be the object of the quest.

Predation precedes the quest.

Wandering precedes predation.

*

Something that wasn't human sought to pass for human.

An animality surrounded by animals went into raptures, fell over backwards, died, named, became monstrous.

*

I mention the global, financial *whatever-it's-worth*, in which value is caught in a dizzying whirl and spins around ever faster, like a shaman in a trance.

*

European humanity is anti-human.

*

In August 1945, the first *Homo sapiens sapiens* was irradiated.

In February 1997, the first animal was cloned.

The Vestals at Rome were the guardians of (1) fire, and (2) the *fascinus*.[†]

The people of the twentieth century abandoned
(1) atomic guardianship (ignition, explosion), and
(2) genetic guardianship (fascination, the code).

*

A kind of violent, social, technical dominion, a high-amplitude, long-term, garrulous dominion, replete with waste and ruins, born of the imitation of hunted animals and of the observation, then exploitation, of the phenomena of nature, has gradually substituted itself for the erratic, low-amplitude, immediate, virtually self-cleansing, biological reign of the plant and animal species over the earth.

CHAPTER 31

Stone is a hardened mud. Caves are hardened mud. I seek neither stone nor hardness.

White horses are not horses.[†] I am after mud.

Let this be understood: my hermitage is not solid. Nothing can be built upon what I write.

The hand that writes is like the hand panicked by the storm. You have to throw the cargo into the sea when the boat is sinking.

CHAPTER 32

Churches of Leyden

He left as he said he would. Left again. Went to Endegeest. There he moved into a large house with two wings and a long garden with a little orchard at the end of it.

All around, endless meadows.

After the meadows and fields, right on the horizon, rising up above the tufts of grass, the little steeples of the churches of Leyden stood out.

The temples wherein dwell God and his saints mingled with the pistils of the flowers.

The weathercocks on top of them looked like the barbs that grow on thistles and prick you.

CHAPTER 33

Post tenebras

Of the Calvinists' maxim *Post tenebras lux*, I retain only the first two words.[†]

Something that does not dazzle enlightens those who were engendered sexually and have developed in the half-light.

A little kernel of human beings whispers, '*Post tenebras*.'

On the edge of the terraces, with the blackbirds, we preserve something that isn't blackness in the dark, but isn't light in the day either.

*

It isn't clear when clean and dirty became separated in human societies and consciousness.

When did the corpse appear and the anguished need to remove it from sight?

Inhumation preceded *sapiens sapiens*.

Art is among the oldest prehuman practices and is much older than money, into which nothing from the sphere of art can be converted.

Art is the sempiternal contemporary of a separation that does not subordinate it.

It was born before the disjunctive, arborescent filiations became fixed between man and beast, between the social and the asocial, order and disorder, the adorned and the repellent, the heavenly and the hellish, life and death, form and non-form.

The sacred, the unclean, that which defiles and that which must be set apart (or concealed from view) are not clearly distinct.

The sacred has never been so omnipotent as it is in modern societies. We have never before separated ourselves to this same extent from corpses, menstrual blood, spit, snot, urine, faeces, belches, scabs, dust and mud.

We are all obsessive priests in our kitchens.

We are insane tyrants in our bathrooms.

It is difficult to dissociate the notions of hygiene, morality, sacrifice, thought, racism and war. We constantly have an eye out for the other, for what is socially or sensorially unclassified, for parasites, mice, saliva, for what is marginal, for what lives in the interstices (spiders and field mice or scorpions are never either inside or outside), self-taught academics, mammalian fish, Christian Jews, single mothers, undrinkable water and border dwellers—whether in terms of national territories or the body—sperm, pins, nail clippings, sweat, phlegm, ghosts, phobias, fantasies (which hack through the wall that should separate wakefulness from sleep). Art is a parasitical production.

The one who brings forth that which did not exist until he came along is of the realm of the inappropriate.

He is out of place. This is the very definition of dirt: something is out of place. A shoe is clean when it is on a floor. It is dirty as soon as you put it on the tablecloth among the flowers, the silverware and the neatly aligned glasses.

*

Money is a future-dependent ritual of exchange. It is a shared faith, the evaluation of which proliferates into a system of equivalences.

Art, in its asystasis, is the Other of that which 'takes' in the form of a system.

Works of art are all at war with this more recent—competing, facile, credulous—mode of representation.

Creative artists represent a danger for the sect that has extended its fanatical belief to the whole earth: they play with things symbolic. They cannot organize themselves in accordance with that order, they do not subscribe to that faith. They are deceivers. The wheeler dealers do not like this proliferation which complicates trade, and the bankers are wary of the impiety which threatens to dissolve the medium of that trade.

Creative artists have no plan.

They go they know not where.

Upstanding businessmen don't like the tricks Reynard the Fox is constantly playing on them. The anxiety of investors is religious: what would happen if human beings stopped believing in the exchange-value of money? The great banking buildings that have invaded the earth would be so many temples of Angkor Wat, buried under tropical creepers and jungle cries, with all trace of men's ancient faith in equivalence expunged.

*

Nowadays, those called creative artists are overrated.

Creative works are underrated.

Oddly enough, while the *res publica* has become entirely profane and venal, time, otherness, nature, history, the sacred and even language—or, at least, linguistic representation—have become *res privata*.

*

Ernest Renan was reluctant to accept the money due to him from the sale of his first book.[†] He couldn't see any common measure between the expression of thoughts, the abandonment of faith and the coin of the realm. His sisters had to intervene to point out to him that, though it did not necessarily entail acceptance, this absence of connection also gave no grounds for refusal.

Similarly, Émile Auguste Chartier wrote pieces in the *Dépêche De Rouen* without taking any payment for them.[†] He said he was a teacher and what that brought him was sufficient for his needs. He took his pseudonym—Alain—from the barbarian people the *Alani*. In January 1911, he agreed to a contract with the commercial department of the *Éditions de la Nouvelle revue française* on the express condition that he received no royalties on the books he published with them.

*

An accelerating obsolescence characterizes those products most involved in the commerce between individuals, images and things—namely, things journalistic, promotional, audiovisual, industrial and political.

This marks a comeback for the trigger-finger style of the Roman emperors. The princes of ancient

Rome were happy to express their approval only so as to experience the omnipotent, sadistic joy of withdrawing that approval immediately with a gesture of the thumb.

This imperial digit was the 'manifest'.

To be more precise, *manifestus* was the Roman word applied to the crime in which the culprit was caught red handed. The Roman world imagines the murderer being *seized by the hand of the accuser*.

In Latin, something is 'manifest' when the crime is visible in it.

The law of the ancient Fathers was based on the *mancipatio*: that which the hand holds as its own.

I regard two classes of entities that are held in the hand as contradictory: the page of a book covered in black letters that signify things and a banknote representing the equivalent in value of those things. At all events, the hand holds them as its own.

To employ bygone terms, I range the *volumen* (a scroll) against the *stips* (a bronze coin).

On the one side, the person who knows his letters, the *litteratus*, the scholar; on the other, the person for whom the *stips* is destined: the stipendiary, the prostitute.

The Roman polarization between persons of rank (*classicus*) and persons of no rank, between *littera* and slavery, between *otium* and *negotium*, is one single distinction.

*

Moneta was a *monitory* temple.

Language has only our bodies for shelter. *Homo* is defined by that alone: the language-using animal.

In the Roman world, Moneta was the temple that *diverted* man from language by *warning* of the omnipotence of the gods.

The *templum* of Juno Moneta was filled with the sound of the smiths hammering.[†]

Money, like the silent exchange it ushers in, like the image, would wish language to leave us.

Admittedly, written language is not definitional of the human species. It defines only the civilizations that assembled themselves around earlier languages deprived of human bodies to speak them.

Dead languages, like Sumerian for the men of Akkad. Like the unpronounceable language that is termed literary, but is in fact transliterating, for the scholars of China, Korea and Japan. Like Hebrew for the Jews, when Cyrus the Messiah allowed them to return from Babylon and they had lost the ordinary usage of it. Like Latin for all the countries of Christian Eurasia.

*

There are supercorporeal bodies that are called anti-bodies. They are imageless. They are without echo. No dreamer dreams them. No world contains them. It is said that they write.

CHAPTER 34

Perditos

Of some human beings we say that they are lost. *Perditos*. They are like holes burned by acid in ordinary social life.

CHAPTER 35

At the end of Antoine Arnauld's interview with Saint-Cyran in the keep at Vincennes on 8 May 1642, Monsieur de Saint-Cyran concluded by telling Monsieur Arnauld, 'We must go where God leads and not be in any way cowardly.'

After 8 May, there was no further communication between them. They never saw one another again.

CHAPTER 36

The Barefoot Teacher

The mysterious sermon of the no less mysterious Barefoot Teacher (*Barfusser Lesemeister*) opens with these words: *Tenebra Deus est. Tenebra in anima post omnem lucem relicta* (God is a darkness. He is the sudden darkness that invests the soul when all light is gone).[†]

CHAPTER 37

Terror [†]

Ludwig Wittgenstein was the theorist of the disappearance of language.

The *Sprachlosigkeit* [speechlessness] was the name given in Germany to the 1914–18 war.

The inexpressibility in words of what was experienced at the front—not to speak of the *Propaganda* that held sway on the home front.

Language ceased to be a bridge between Ego and Cosmos.

The desire to speak was lost in the trenches.

*

In 1936, Thierry Maulnier founds *Combat*.[†] In that magazine, Robert Brasillach reports the following:

'When I hear talk of culture,' Mr Goering said one day, 'I take my revolver from its holster.' Claude Orland[†] (who had not yet become Claude Roy) takes the view that the warmongers aren't Mussolini, Hitler, Salazar and Franco, but Blum, Roosevelt, Stalin and Churchill. Maurice Blanchot[†] publishes a long article entitled 'Terrorism as a Method of Public Safety.' Terror is an eighteenth-century word. It is the last message of that century. Then comes 1871. Over a two-year period, Paris was besieged by the Germans and Paris was besieged by the French. In one week, 35,000 men, women, old people and children were executed. More people were transported to the colonies and into penal servitude than during the whole history of the Republic.

In three days, the Thiers government was responsible for more victims than the Terror produced in three years.

From the start of the First World War to the end of the Second, 70 million human beings were massacred.

The word 'terrorism' belongs to the criminal law. Society defines it as political criminality that does not seek to establish or re-establish public order but to disrupt it spectacularly. The word has rarely been claimed as such by historical actors: it was invoked by the French revolutionaries and by European movements of the fascist Right before 3 September 1939.

*

Writing is entirely political.

Vercors: Between the occupier and the writer, no exchange, no words, no contact, no payment of wages and no communication are conceivable.[†]

I try to keep to this rule laid down by Vercors. The person who writes is someone who tries to redeem what has been pawned. To take language out of hock. To break the dialogue. To desubordinate domestication. To extricate himself from brotherhood and fatherland. To undo all religious bonds.

*

Once it has become song, the appeal contained in the cry is no longer addressed to anyone.

The arts are not destined, as history is, to organize forgetfulness. Nor to give meaning to meaning's Other. Nor to besmirch and swallow up the bygone days of the earth. Nor here and now to abolish time's Elsewhere. Nor to proscribe the languages that predate all natural languages. Nor to wall up the Open. You have to be a Nazi to think that art is a decorative lie. You have to be a Communist to see art as recreation. You have to be a bourgeois liberal to think it amuses. Only in totalitarian regimes is art conceived as an aestheticization of subjection, a creation of legends out of the past, a constant faking-up of the coming and passing hour. The artist cannot take part in the operation of the human community at the very same time as he is striving to detach himself from it. Nor is it even for him to receive wages in exchange for his work. He is closer to mourning than to pay. Less forgetful than voluntary memory. Less self-interested than money in trade. It is not the function of art to deny the Other of the social.

*

The individual is like the wave rising to the surface of the water. That wave cannot separate itself entirely and very quickly falls back into the interdependent mass that engulfs it. It always sinks back into the irresistible movement of the tide that bears it along. But why not rise up again and again and again?

CHAPTER 38

Over the shoulder of the ferryman leaning all his weight on his boathook in the Bassin du Roi at Le Havre and far in the distance where the clouds meet the sea, the outlines of the British ships were visible, threatening the coasts with a hundred years' war.

CHAPTER 39

After he was let out of his prison in 1643, Monsieur de Saint-Cyran evoked the vanities of the world, along the same lines as painters had come to represent them in their pictures:

half-filled wine glasses;

red and brown lutes;

off-white playing cards and candles;

lemon peel hanging over the edges of tables;

mirrors with reflections;

mirrors without reflections.

He said he had happily gone without all these objects in his cell.

You can get along without even the image of what you do not have.

Dreams provide a sufficient substitute (*Ersatz*) for all the body is deprived of.

*

It was also in prison that Monsieur de Saint-Cyran penned this page:

> For after the greed for wealth, honours and worldly pleasures has been destroyed, there arise in the soul—out of those ruins—other honours, other wealth, other pleasures that are not of this visible world, but of the invisible world.

It is dreadful to think that, after destroying within us the visible world, with all its trappings, as much as it can be destroyed on this earth, another invisible one is immediately born, a world more difficult to destroy than the first.

Saint-Cyran speaks of the vanity of books that are merely books. Of gods that are mere phantasms. Of ideas that are merely desires.

He adds that there were in eternity three restrictions, in addition to the one concerning the number of the elect. He knew this from his experience in the cell the king had thrown him into.

Before my imprisonment, I used to think that behind the visible world there was another world. Now, having emerged from the shadow in which the king chose to place me to rest my eyes, I think that behind the invisible world, there is yet another, which alone is real.

Beyond the arts of the senses, there is the art of language, in which all symbols are renewed, because that art invents them.

And, behind language, what precedes it is not silence, which is merely the opposite of natural language—that is to say, its contemporary—but the realm behind the invisible.

*

We knew life before the sun dazzled our eyes and we understood something in it that could neither be read nor seen.

*

The definition of modern art was provided by Pierre Guillard on 11 August 1932. Pierre Guillard had studied science and was by profession an engineer. He rushed at Millet's *Angelus* and stabbed the canvas several times. He was overcome by the attendants. At the police station to which the Louvre's attendants took him, he declared:

'At least they'll talk about me.'

Self-promotion, the refusal of subjection and the hatred, in all that has been, of the *this was*—this is the triple thesis of modern art.

An allergic reaction to dependence, the discrediting of what went before and the elimination of *the erstwhile*—these are the arguments of progress.

Guillard damaged the peasant's trousers and wounded the stooping woman in the arm. The sky was irreparable.

*

It was never so cold on this earth as in the century when neoteny was interrupted.

Larvae even stopped their metamorphosing.

The universe teems with phantoms or poorly colourized, poorly dubbed reflections;

as they age, colours overflow their outlines;

gradually, the ancient languages are becoming desynchronized on the flesh of my lips.

*

It is possible that the beauty of the arts as arts began to die in the eighteenth century, at the point when terror was being born. The sublime according to Kant was in the human mind. The sublime according to the inventor of the sublime (according to Longinus) was in nature. Nature now ceases to harbour its own strength within itself. Man begins to contemplate himself like a Narcissus loving himself to excess, to the point of disfigurement.

*

It is not certain that works of art have ever been awaited. When they happen to be greeted with favour, we discover it was not to *them* that the hospitality was extended.

La Fontaine's *Fables* met with immediate favour but were, at the same time, poorly understood.[†] They were so easily learned in cold classrooms only because their painful meanings—full of religious impiety and social mistrust—were not commented upon.

At times also, hateful vehemence and prohibition have formed the welcoming committee.

To tell the truth, however tiny it may be, a work of art adds to the totality of things something that was scarcely present before. Things that should not normally have occurred are a source of embarrassment. Even the return of a tradition may be intrusive and, as it were, disruptive. A second point makes art an embarrassment: not only does it augment the unpredictable but it hates death. Artists are murderers of death. Hence it is normal that they should be punished by those who make it their business either to administer death or to add to it.

*

Mimicry roams through nature, the product of a pre-human fascination in which the eye seeks to devour what it loves.

Carnivorousness is a fascination in action.

It was in ferocious fascination that symbolization carried out its first trials.

Even between butterflies and flowers a ferocious exchange lingers, detaches itself, overflies its own form, wanders off, comes back, embeds itself.

Desire is always subjugated.

St Thomas used the word *abalietas*.[†] With this, he wanted to show that any human creature, born of another, founded upon another, instructed by another, functioned only *ab alio*, only thanks to— and at the random mercy of—an irreducible alterity. We are merely derivatives. Language, identity, body, memory—everything in us is derivative. The foundation of *ego* within us is much more fragile, much less substantial than our origins from the other, *ab alio*; more fragile than what is passed on by our families, than our social education, our traditions, our moral religion or our linguistic allegiance. Fascination precedes identity. Within self-esteem, there is much more internalized *socius* than subjective positioning. Nowhere has there ever been much of that *love of self* that is preached. It is always a fascinated imprint. A product of fascination—the attribution of a name, a mother's gaze, the reproduction of an ancestor, etc. There is no self-resemblance.

*

What was thought, what was thought noetically, what was thought philologically, what was thought etymologically (I am calling to mind a perception that is *not completely imaginary*) became *unimaginable*. Now, what becomes unimaginable seems no longer to exist.

*

It is the dominant morality that defines what is marginal. A morality in which what once was symbolic has become imaginary (an image on paper or an image on a screen, or an image in fantasies and dreams) cannot incorporate imageless modes (literature and music) into its system of representation.

The marginalization of writers and musicians is sure and enduring.

The prestige of painters, architects, models, film stars, politicians, TV presenters, men of violence and those who die 'on camera' is assured. It has been attested since 1933. There is no point battling on in a lost cause. All one can do is transform social marginality into dissidence. All one can do is transform a marginality of status into a diriment anchoritism.

*

Those who try to collude with the system will become images.

They will grow pale.

They will pale as suddenly as the photographs you expose to the sunlight on the breakfast table.

Baked and curled up by noon.

Hopeless shreds by the time of the nightly dew-fall that brings the morrow.

*

Time was, in the ancient civilizations, one of which invented democracy and the other the republic (and pitted the two against each other), when human speech and action were so tightly bound together that the world was seen as governed by language.

Regina rerum oratio.[†]

Nowadays, when the forum has become a *templum*—a *contemplum* of moving images—the world believes itself governed by images in motion.

Regina rerum imago.

*

The objects of the desires that stirred the loins of Caesar and Antony were, admittedly, depraved. But Cleopatra was a living object. In his triumphal processions, Caesar dragged Cleopatra along on an ox-drawn cart. Vercingetorix followed behind, tugging on his chain. A placard portrayed a dying Brutus modelled in wax. And, lastly, there was a giraffe— preceded only by lictors stamping along the streets and carrying the *fascis*.

*

In old Japan, the palanquin was called a 'silhouette box'.

*

The guards push the men into the blood-soaked arena that is now bathed in light; comments are passed on the ways of the animals and the rapes of the Christian women; the priests' and augurs' regrets are whispered, the commendations of the *vicarii* reported; there is applause for the prowess of the mercenaries.

They speak, but all are merely pretending to speak: they are watching out for the point of weakness.

They are all enraptured by the kill.

Lions with gazelles, raptors with lizards, cats with mice and so on.

*

A half-dead Narcissus reigns. An ancient rationality, once local and mercantile, now global and aimless, governs his gaze. His thoughts are entirely absorbed by his reflection, if we can still speak of thought in his case: he is a gaze, a screen, a reflection. The gaze seeks out the reflection. The reflection seeks the screen. The screen seeks the gaze.

*

Everyone's gaze fixed on no one's reflection.

CHAPTER 40

All the cheerfulness had gone from my table. Everyone was lost in personal reminiscence.

The youngest were still discovering that sorry, private, stinking inner swamp, in which you ultimately drown.

I went out.

On the gravel path, I turned round suddenly and looked at the house as though I were seeing it for the first time.

I looked at the house, the garden, the pond, the box trees.

Then I looked down towards the green forest, which was gradually being invaded by the mist rising from the river.

I walked away.

Lancelot roamed.

CHAPTER 41

Rousseau had a friend called Monsieur de Merveilleux who lived at Soleure.[†]

CHAPTER 42

The Brouette

On the death of Louis XIV in 1715, Mademoiselle de Joncoux went the length and breadth of Paris, attempting to secure the release of the Jansenists who had been imprisoned and persecuted by the late king.

She knocked on every door, wherever it might be; in the corners of church porches, beneath the colonnades of palaces, in the antechambers of lords and in the private apartments of the ministers of state.

In all these perpetual comings and goings, she did not use a carriage; nor even a sedan chair. She sat in a *brouette*.[†]

People called it a *brouette*, a *berouette* or a *vinaigrette*.

In those days they sang.

As soon as she was seated, Mademoiselle de Joncoux began to read.

A man who stood facing her (or, at least, facing her open book) pushed the *vinaigrette* in which Mademoiselle de Joncoux sat, as comfortably as she could, on a folding stool affixed to a floor made of two planks of wood that had been screwed together to form an arch over the single wheel.

Mademoiselle de Joncoux didn't stop reading for more than ten years.

She had had a grey roof installed.

She always wore dresses the colour of tree bark, so that they would be as dark as possible.

The only finery she permitted herself was a brown headscarf, which she termed her 'indulgence'. She was thin.

When she reached her destination, she would hold out a bony hand in the dull, pale air characteristic of the capital of the French.

The man pushing her would take her hand and pull on it.

A black woollen garment would be seen exiting from its box.

It was Port-Royal's last surviving soul who planted her shoe on the cobbles and teetered in the mud, warily grasping her book in her hand.

CHAPTER 43

There are ways of saying things that send a shudder through people.

Others that wound.

There are ways of saying things that still wound in the memory, even after the death of those who used them.

These voices and intonations form what we may call 'the family'.

There are ways of saying things that intoxicate one's breath with dead or muffled voices. But voices or echoes that do not emanate directly from those dead. Originating in a breath that isn't directly ancestral. Or that assail the throat with a secret voice, an orality more concealed than vocal resonance—lower than a murmur—and make you want to weep.

Such are books.

The totality of books (this totality excludes all the volumes in which orality or society have not been sacrificed) forms what we may call literature, which is an afamilial, not directly genealogical family, an asocial society.

*

Interior is a comparative for everything that is internal.

Intimate—*intime*—is the superlative.

A voice so *intimate* that it is no longer even conveyable on the air.

That it is no longer of the same order as the breath in the body.

*

Books that can be said to be *touched by the reflection of the sun, of which they know nothing,* are even more silent than purely literary ones. They are like the name of a person one loves, but a name one cannot utter, since his children would then learn who their real father is, though he does not know it himself.

*

Books without pictures have become like the endowed Masses of old. The pious would pay, during their lifetimes, for church services to be said in perpetuity to ensure their survival. They had in their time left purses full of *gold louis from the year 1640* with their lawyers. Or they had offset the cost of these services against still active estates bequeathed to an ecclesiastical living for its use or profit.

Offices were sung for no one present.

Unmarried men in black robes earned this money from the hands of corpses, then from the bones of skeletons, then from the dust of hands that no longer existed anywhere.

Just as the priest would say Mass into the void, just as the organist would climb to the organ loft for a memory with no living connections in this world, so too a book is addressed to eyes that the person writing it does not see.

*

These were extraordinary revenues from the Erstwhile in its purest state. They declined abruptly from the early eighteenth century onwards.

Ransomings of the dead that established fewer and fewer Erstwhiles.

These were still continuations of the first human burials.

A piece of good fortune that has already occurred silently comes towards us once again.

We must welcome its gushing ruin, its ruinous generosity, its halo of trembling, invisible fervour.

Caesar devotes a brief page to the warriors of Gaul. He writes: Everything the dead man is supposed to have been fond of . . . is placed upon his pyre.[†]

*

The Melusinian taboo on language is the finest of themes.

Petrifying, paralyzing beauty is the only beauty. The beauty that precedes the worlds of men. The fascinating beauty suddenly recognized by stilled beasts.

For melancholics, aphasics and mutes, for those being born, for children, dreamers, true musicians, and erotophiles, for the phantasmagorical, for writers, lovers and the dying, it is the sole form.

*

To experience, through thinking, something that is striving for expression, before one even knows it—this is doubtless what the movement of writing is. To write, on the one hand, with this word that is forever on the tip of your tongue and, on the other, with the whole of language as it slips through your fingers. This is called burning, at the dawn of discovery.

I burn! I burn! To reignite all that follows with the intensity of things at their beginning.

*

To bring all things out of the anterior darkness. *To set the lost afire with loss—this, properly speaking, is what it is to read.* To procure its eleventh-hour colour for everything that is burning out.

Re-finding the dawn absolutely everywhere is a way of living.

Reconstituting birth in every autumn, hailing the lost in the unfindable, raising up the ceaseless, unforeseeable other in the irruption of the first time, for there are no others.

Being born.

Language still endowed with silence is the nest. Just as the visible endowed with darkness is the dream.

Then the letter that points silently to the lost song, and behind the lost song, to the old lost hearing of it, is literature.

Then the cave that reproduces the involuntary or celestial images, as though it were still a question of dreams, is painting.

The darkness of the cave is the dream made mountain.

The cave wall is the human skin inside the eyelid.

And this nest, made from fragments of twig snatched one by one from the surrounding space and from bits of string that misfortune accumulates for survival purposes, occupies the entire volume of the human head while it is still inventing, just before it finds its words. When it is thinking before it remembers within time. When it finds more than when it knows. When it writes more than when it recognizes.

When it climaxes more than when it writes.

When it desires more than when it climaxes.

Literature consists entirely in this silent prelude. In this book-nest. In this *Urszene* full of images no one dares express.[†]

Written books are the secretariat of the secret.

The two great discoveries or inventions: the cave in the mountain, the book in language.

*

For it was caves that gave rise to craniums.

It was monasteries that saved the West.

Humanity owes more to reading than to weapons. In India too. In Tibet too. In Japan too. In Iceland too. In China, the reading of the written word was the very foundation of civilization. When everyone has stopped reading, literature will be prized once again. That experience will recreate its hermitages, so much is it the case that no other human experience can compete with it.

The most de-socializing experience there ever was.

The most anchoritic.

So much so that its history never transited from country to country. It passed from monastery to monastery.

Passed from monk to monk.

Passed from *monos* to *solus*.

From one lone being to another.

CHAPTER 44

On 9 October 1989, I left Bergheim.

Secret societies of free men are set to become tinier and tinier. They are reduced now almost to individuals. My friends are increasingly dear to me and fewer and fewer in number. Ammianus Marcellinus reports that when the emperor offered the empire freedom, it was seen as a lethal trap. The people said:

'He's offering us our freedom in order to ruin us.'

The leading citizens gathered their clients together and declared:

'Freedom is a way Caesar has found of enslaving us.'

So much did they aspire to tyranny, so much did they wish to maintain the ascendancy of the gods and preserve the authority of family relations that there wasn't a single man willing to take advantage of the possibility of desiring and taking, of hiding, of moving, of living the way a bird flits, pecks, hops and turns its head this way and that.

They all refused to be free.

*

Freedom had been the highest value in ancient Rome. A value so unconditional and non-negotiable that under the entire period of monarchy, and throughout the republic and empire, fathers were not allowed to deprive their children of it.

Fathers had the right of life and death over their children.

But even when they gave them up to others, even when they sold them, even when they banished them from the family home, even when they exposed them, even when they cut their throats, they could not take away their freedom.

*

The Senate's envoys found Cincinnatus bare-armed, digging over the four acres of land he owned on the banks of the Tiber.

With a woollen cloth he wiped the sweat from his brow.

He stripped naked on the beaten-earth floor of his cabin; he rubbed with straw at the mud that had dried on his body; he wound his toga around his thighs and his torso.

He went outside.

He climbed into the boat that took him to the Forum. He defeated the Aequi at Algidus Mons. After sixteen days, Cincinnatus abdicated as dictator and went back to his digging.

*

When Yao governed the state, Po-cheng Tsu-kao received a fief from him. Yao handed on the state to Shun who passed it to Yu.[†] Po-cheng Tsu-kao therefore gave up his fief and took up the plough. Yu went to see him and found him busy ploughing his field. I like these meetings where time and space are of no account.

Yu approached Po-cheng Tsu-kao respectfully and said:

'Master, the sovereign Yao gave you a fief. Why do you now wish to give it up to plough your field?'

'I am not *envisaging* giving it up. I have given it up.'

'That doesn't greatly alter the question I'm asking. Why?'

'Yao no longer reigns. You do.'

'I don't think it right to answer me like that,' murmured Yu.

'Out of what must be said, I don't know what is right,' replied Po-cheng Tsu-kao.

'Perhaps ploughing fields has addled your head,' suggested Yu.

'I don't know whether ploughing my poor field has addled my head, but I've a feeling that in the days when Yao reigned, the people didn't give him much thought. Now you reward a great deal and punish a great deal, but the clean is not separated from the dirty, nor man from woman, nor evil from good, nor stranger from brother, nor names from things. This is the beginning of disorders that will last a long time. Why do you not go? Leave me in peace! I would ask you to interrupt my work no further.'

This is what Po-cheng Tsu-kao replied to celebrate Emperor Yu's accession to the empire.

*

On Tuesday, 10 October, I closed up the flat in Stuttgart.

On Wednesday, 11 October 1989, I left Karlsruhe where I had been reading in the yellow park. I arrived at Frankfurt. Between the solitude of the one who writes and the solitude of the one who reads, there is much that cements the two.

An enormous fair at which only cheques are read. This is the festival of the go-betweens. While the beasts cry out as they are sent to slaughter, the breeders count the blood money. We are the primary sector. I muttered, 'Don't interrupt me!'

I whispered more and more quietly, 'Don't interrupt me!'

I was writing.

We are the cattle.

*

Why, one April day in 1994, a day of fine weather and dazzling sunshine, did I suddenly quicken my step as I was coming out of the Louvre? A man speeds up as he crosses the Seine, looks, beneath the arches of the Pont-Royal, at the water shimmering over its full expanse with a gleaming whiteness, sees the clear blue sky above the rue de Beaune, runs up to a large wooden door on the rue Sébastien-Bottin, pushes it open and resigns at a stroke from all his functions.

*

You cannot be both a warder and an escapee.

*

This is the first argument.

Benedict Spinoza called the Dutch the last of the barbarians (*ultimi barbarorum*).

This is Letter 50: The mind, insofar as it uses reason, is not the province of the state, but of itself.

Spinoza ranged the friend, the *carus*, against the crowd, the *vulgus*, seeing them as two opposite poles.

He wrote: We do not expect freedom from those for whom slavery has become their principal trade.

*

What the individuals who feel part of the collectivities in which they work are looking for is fusion with a larger body. They rediscover the old joy that came from abandoning oneself to a containing vessel. They surrender the subjectivity the learning of language brings to each of us, and renounce also the problematical privileges that come of being identified by a name. They give themselves up to the desires of others; they delight in the many, repetitive, fetishistic, obsessive, sempiternal joys of the masochists. To cite Ammianus Marcellinus, they prefer the restoration of a known tyrant (who humiliates them within the bounds of the laws they have laid down to limit excessive injury)

to unpredictable anxiety;

or to the absence of a father figure;

or to his contempt;

or to loneliness.

*

All communities seek social recognition as a sign emitted from farther afield than the external space, from farther than the air of the atmosphere, from before birth: a sign of belonging. Bears, skylarks, women, homosexuals, the sick, beggars, wanderers, musicians, painters, writers and saints—do not announce yourselves to the political authorities.

Do not demand justice from the law court or meaning from the state.

This is the second argument: the state is, by definition, without foundation, like law itself.

It is founded on a violent death, in just the same way as the scapegoat creates the god.

As a martyr creates the tyrant.

As Damocles creates Dionysius.

*

The rejection of social belonging is a thing that has been condemned by every human group. Such a condemnation is the basis of every myth.

Like the lovers' passion, which shatters the codified, hierarchical exchange between the members of the group to ensure its reproduction.

Homer wrote: An *apolis* individual is a civil war.

The old bard meant by this that any man without a city is a germ of civil war.

Herodotus wrote: No isolated human individual can be sufficient unto himself.

To quote his exact word, he cannot be *autarkes*.

The Bible says, 'Woe to him that is alone.' A solitary man is a dead man.

But this is wrong. This is always what society says. In all oral literature, the narrator is society. All myths, everywhere on earth, declare that there is no happy love, in order to preserve exchanges between clans and genealogical alliances.

But this is wrong.

For there have been forbidden lovers who have known happiness.

There have been lone figures, hermits, wanderers, outsiders, shamans, marginals and solitaries, who have been the happiest of people.

*

There have always been individuals who have broken with the families with which they were affiliated or the clans to which they belonged.

The decision to get away from everyone else, the choice of outsider status emerges the moment the first family unit appears among animal groups.

171

*

Since the dawn of time, springs frequented caves and caves attracted viviparous creatures. They sheltered there. They came back after the glaciers had hollowed out the caves as they abandoned them.

CHAPTER 45

I was walking in the street, forehead bowed, head full of intense, futile thoughts. Suddenly, I felt someone push me violently in the back. I fell forward so quickly that I didn't have time to reach out my hands. I fell right on my head. I felt someone's presence very near me. I raised my head and looked him up and down.

I could feel my teeth were bleeding.

He was a very handsome, pale young man, wearing a sort of cassock. He had a little yellow *grenade** in his hand and he was holding it up to my eyes. I wanted to touch my chin, which was hurting, but I was immediately kneed in the mouth, which made me cry out weakly. He was wearing big high-ankle trainers.

'Don't move!' he said softly.

I wasn't moving: my eyes were watering with pain.

He put out his hand. He took the wallet from my inside pocket. He took the money that was in it and let the wallet drop near my face. He went off without running.

I could see him: he was leaving, but without running.

I tried to get up on all fours. Suddenly, I felt hands on my back once more. My spirits sank again. And these hands were tugging at me. I turned around: it was an old woman trying to get me back on my feet. She was pulling me. At the same time, she was asking,

'Do you want me to call the police?'

'Absolutely not', I murmured, suddenly panicking.

'Why?' asked the old woman.

In my dream I was crying. I said: 'I don't want them to take me to Drancy.'[†]

CHAPTER 46

We must see things this way: the hunter is death. Man is merely the prey.

The secession is now total.

Men of letters can no longer stand alongside the vassals.

The Brahmin and the Rajah no longer speak to one another.

For the first time, the form of a society is opposed to the existence of a literature.

Neutrality in the way a society might be organized belongs now among the *impossibilia*.

Neuter, in the strictest sense, means depolarized.

Depolarized social polarization is civil war.

This isn't even religious civil war, this isn't even a rising of the princes.

A state that is no longer a more or less inhibited civil war is no longer a state.

A market that has become a single market is no longer a market war but a depolarized market.

A non-polar exchange, an international financial system without either referent or *alter* are *impossibilia*.

*

On the two values advocated by the old English colonies that have been settled for the last five hundred years on New World soil: puritanism and optimism.

These two values can be summed up in a single one: a dismaying joviality.

Respect for money, industry, profit, fertility, reproduction, women, health, light, children, learning, victory, baseball and vitality—this is the credo. This in no way corresponds to what the Athenians had been trying to refer to two thousand four hundred years earlier when they invented the name *democracy*.

*

Freedom of conscience wasn't among the luggage carried on the *Mayflower*.

Democracy never crossed the Atlantic.

But how could the ideas of the *Aufklärung* and the French Revolution be hoisted aboard a ship in 1620?

Here is what the puritan Fathers who landed in Massachusetts Bay brought in the chests they wedged one by one upon the muddy shore: sin; the prohibition of tobacco; stovepipe hats; the disapproval of novels; the eradication of any inner life; a ban on playing cards; flared boots; black clothing; firearms; the prohibition of finery; the prohibition of perfumes; the prohibition of ribbons and lace; the prohibition of obscene images; the missionary extermination of the prehistoric, post-Siberian tribes that had arrived eight thousand years before through the strait discovered by Vitus Bering; the Bible; a ban on wearing gloves; fat, serious faces; hatred of the body; bare, white hands; racism; slavery for the blacks bought on the coasts of Africa; witch hunting; Joseph R.

McCarthy, Senator for Wisconsin, public overseer of everyone's thinking; Texan Prosecutor Kenneth Starr, Son of God.

*

On Saturday, 10 October 1998, the American Senate unanimously adopted the International Religious Freedom Act.

The burden of that Act is that sanctions, commercial or financial, will be imposed on any country convicted of religious persecution, an independent commission being tasked with monitoring the damaging effects of atheism.

On Sunday, 11 October 1998, Michael Horowitz hailed it as a 'great victory over the view of the world inherited from the Enlightenment' (Hudson Institute).

*

In 1637, Père Joseph said to Richelieu: 'When I look upon the cities, forests, seas and glaciers, I begin to believe the world is a fable and we have lost our reason.'

In Paris, Richelieu called his lute player and bade him play the chaconne entitled *The Last Kingdom*.

He then played *The Shadows that Wander*, the main theme of which François Couperin borrowed, calling it *Les Ombres errantes—Roving Shadows—*in his last book for harpsichord.

At the same point in history, George Fox was developing his Society of Friends.

The *Augustinus* appeared.[†]

*

One day, Richelieu said of Saint-Cyran, 'The man is Basque and you can tell. Steamy temper and vapid thinking.'

*

It happened to be at Leuven that Saint-Cyran got to know Jansenius. They climbed into a post-chaise and the two of them went to stay in Saint-Cyran's

Campiprat residence at Bayonne, which fronted on to the beauty and violence of the Atlantic Ocean.

They nurtured the dream of a tiny group of men who would revive the origins of Christian thought as it was in Nero's empire.

For relaxation, they played battledore and shuttle cock, becoming great exponents of the game. Madame de Hauranne said she had seen them make 3,223 consecutive shots without missing.

Jansenius said to Saint-Cyran, 'We are saltpetre that burns without leaving a residue. The earth is a closed field in which powers and desires confront one another. We withdraw into gardens of eighty *mines*.[†] The god we adore has narrower and narrower arms. We are in the year 300. You are Metrodorus and I an ardent Epicurus. I am seeking Metrodorus' daughter.'

To which Monsieur de Saint-Cyran was moved to reply: 'The shuttlecock is the whole of present time rising towards the sky in the accumulated air that gives it its depth and colour. There is a shadow which those who run swiftest do not cast upon the ground.'

*

Our societies,

fleeing suffering, the negative, fear, impatience, the tragic, melancholy, silence, half-darkness and the invisible,

are forsaking sublime civilizations.

They are frightened by the most vertiginous cliffs, fearful in the deepest jungles. They reject the most thrilling, most desirous and finest joys, which always have in them the risk of ruin and death.

*

We must stay close to the gushing spring.

Prae-sentia. The Latin *prae* is the French word *près*: near to, close to.

Everything is a pathway when the *most intimate proximity* approaches.

I would always distrust someone who says *we* when experiencing orgasm.

Without solitude, without the test of time, without the passion for silence, without the excitation and retention of the whole body, without a frightened stumbling, without wandering into a region of shade and invisibility, without memory of animality, without melancholy, without isolation in melancholy, there is no joy.

*

Just as Cincinnatus had only one idea in his head, which was to get back to his fields, so it is with

the hermit and his desert;

the fish and water;

the reader and his book;

the shadow and its corner.

CHAPTER 47

Emily

Charlotte Bronte wrote that Emily was the tallest of the whole family. Always pale and silent, her eyes dark grey or dark blue. She was indescribable: energetic, stocky, vigorous, wild, shy, inflexible, impassioned, melancholic, proud, undemonstrative (except at the piano).

Emily and Ann were like twins: inseparable and silent.

Inseparable as bodies and shadows.

Emily liked very much to be beside ponds, liked tadpoles, frogs and the smell of water.

She also loved her dog Keeper, with whom she often went for walks.

When, in the summer of 1824, the box of soldiers that would become the 'Young Men' arrived at

Haworth, Emily chose the wooden man who seemed 'a grave-looking fellow' and took him as her hero.

For that reason, the four of us named him 'Gravey'.

Of us all, she was *The one who was grave*.

Her reserve seemed the toughest of things—impenetrable. Yet, she was extraordinarily engaging. I have never seen [her] parallel in anything.[†] Stronger than a man, simpler than a child, her nature stood alone. The gifts she demonstrated for music were truly extraordinary; she was no virtuoso and she was not a great musician, but her touch, style and expression were intense.

The touch, style and expression were those of a master absorbed, body and soul, in her art.

She did not hate suffering and bore it quite well. She consented to illness. At the end, about a year after the publication of her book, which went entirely unnoticed, she lost the will to live. She destroyed all that might remain of her. She made haste to leave us. She died on the drawing-room sofa.[†]

CHAPTER 48

History

In 212 BCE, under the emperor Qin Shi-huang, all men of letters spotted in the empire were buried alive.[†]

In 96 CE, the emperor Domitian expelled all the philosophers and philosophy teachers from the Empire: all those who wore the short cloak.

Short cloaks and thought moved off towards the outer reaches of the Empire: to Brittany, Persia, Çatal Höyük and Palmyra.

Damascius at Baghdad learnt Pahlavi.[†]

CHAPTER 49

In the end, the Frankish king Clovis settled in Paris, which he had taken as the seat of his kingdom on his return from the war in Aquitaine.

He died there.

He loved the rustic appearance of this abode, the fact that the emperor Julian had chosen it, the descriptions he had given of it and that had been reported to him, the beauty of the river and the Merovingian curves of its course.[†]

Meanders of the Seine that irresistibly bring to mind the curls of the hair of the Frankish kings, because the sculptors of that time also lent that same appearance to the son of God.

*

Clovis' list: He loved the forests,

    the surrounding vines,

    the fertility of the fields,

    the gentleness of the skies,

    the extreme paleness of everything.

*

He resided in the former palace of Constantius Chlorus on the left bank of the river, opposite the island of Lutetia, along the Roman high road leading to Orleans.[†]

The immense palace gardens were bounded to the east by the Montagne Ste. Geneviève, the river Bièvre and the Roman baths; to the west by the village of Saint-Germain and the sanctuary of Diana.

They contained trees from the time of Camulogenus.[†]

Two dates are to be remembered from Clovis' reign: when he planted fig trees and when he planted almond trees.

He remained faithful to the battle axe of the Istevons and the intact head of hair that was emblematic of strength.

He forbade any Roman name to taint his family tree.

He did not suffer anyone to speak to him of the last king of the Romans, whom he had had beheaded in 486. He died at the age of forty-five. On 1 December 511, his body was sealed in a trapezoid stone sarcophagus.

*

The Frankish idea of the right of asylum is a praiseworthy one. The idea that there are in space intermediate zones that are free of human domination. Places where private vengeance came to a halt and state vengeance was forbidden. Places in nature where not only was humanity proscribed but even the dominion of the gods ceased to apply.

The Franks didn't know that the free areas were also hermitages, with the horse in the stable, the kitchen, the close-mouthed pages.

*

The fascination exerted by the bared sexual organs, like that exerted by works of art—which themselves lay something bare—has to do with the possibility of rekindling a longing—over a distance of millennia—for something that is no more.

They are so many attributes, vestiges, after-effects of a mysterious island from which all originate but to which none returns—an island lost in our distancing from it, in irreducible difference, by age, the passage of time, death, and a fixed, conformist language.

Art, like gestation, like parturition, links us to the past, as do sexuality and passion. This is Gongsun Long's paradox. It so happens that the finger pointing at something not only recedes into the background in the act of indicating, but is also already absent from the name that will be stammered out from the mouth of the child first attempting to indicate that something.

Every work of art is this language at its source. That is to say, it is a world that has become a past.

We can make no distinction between the defence of the works of the past, the defence of sexual pleasure, the defence of written language and the defence of art.

*

Art obeys no temporal order. Like time itself, it has no orientation.

It knows no progress, no accumulation, no eternity, no place, no centre, no capital, no battlefront.

High watermark of time, when time overflows.

A free zone rather than a zone of liberty.

A liberated zone with no truce in force; a strand ceaselessly to be liberated from the expanding earth and the rising sea.

*

A free zone that is the exact opposite of the free zone represented by the PXs at the end of the Second World War.

The little PX in Berlin in Summer 1945.

The one in Tokyo.

And subsequently the big stores of the PXs of the late-1950s American occupations.

P and X were supposed to be the (more or less initial) letters of the name of the Post Exchange store, where the soldiers of the army of occupation could buy chewing gum,

cigarettes,

sweets,

and candy bars.

Big stores followed armies of occupation like rusted bases, ruined airfields, buckled tennis courts, slow dances, racism, cemeteries, television, raw cauliflower, the dollar and hatred.

*

Free zone or *liber asylum*.

There are two accounts relating the conversion of the emperor Constantine to Christianity when he had to give battle at the Milvian Bridge in 312.

Either the emperor glimpsed a letter in the sky that more or less resembled the Greek letter *tau*—a cross set against the sun (Eusebius' account).

Or the emperor saw two letters in a dream. In this second version, the dream called for the leader of the Roman armies to have his soldiers' shields marked with the letter *chi* and an *iota* drawn across it. Then the army would draw its sword (*iota*) from the initial letter of Christos' name (*chr*) and be victorious (Lactantius' account).

The change effected by Constantine was a simple one: he resolved there would no longer be any images on shields and flags.

He would substitute letters for images.

The gods (the images, first, of wild beasts, then of the heroes who tamed them) were transformed into language.

In 312, humanity, for the first time in its history —in the West, on the plain of Saxa Rubra, before the

Milvian Bridge—voluntarily renounced images and devoted not only its life but all of its dreams to *litterae*.

To literature.

This lettered episode lasted from the twelfth year of the fourth century to the fourteenth year of the twentieth. Then the image flickered once again, fascinated once again, and reconquered all its hypnotic power within men's cranial cavities.

*

Solitude, luck, indocility, the risk of death, disintoxication, lucidity, silence, loss, nudity, *anachoresis*, *excessus*, the gift, immediation, anxiety and excitation are forthright values.

All forthright values are secret.

The blind spot preferred to blinkers.

Forthright means asocial.

*

Bishop Gregory began his *History of the Franks* as follows: *Decedente, atque immo potius pereunte ab urbibus gallicanis liberalium cultura litterarum* . . . With literary culture waning or, rather, perishing in the cities of the Gauls, most people cried out in lamentation, saying: '*Vae diebus nostris, quia periit studium litterarum a nobis, nec reperitur in populis, qui gesta praesentia promulgare possit in paginis!*' Woe unto our times, for the study of letters has perished among us. Woe unto this world because we no longer meet anyone who can put down the things that are happening today (*gesta praesentia*) on the written page!

*

Couperin died in 1733.

In 1731, Couperin wrote in his will:

Since scarcely anyone has composed more than I in several genres, I hope my family will find in my Portfolios such things as to make them regret my passing, if indeed regrets serve any purpose after our lives are over. But we must at least have this idea if we are to try to deserve a chimerical immortality, of the kind to which almost all human beings aspire.

Few beliefs can have presented themselves as less credulous. Even Stéphane Mallarmé's staggering last testament does not have this lucidity.

François Couperin, despised by all and having lost even the company of his last pupils, would drink a little wine when evening had fallen. He would sit down in a white day bed and say to himself: 'In days gone by, I fought in some battle or other near Soissons or Belleu. I asked the shades for a part of their shade. I fought as best I could against the Franks. I composed *Les Chemises blanches* and *Les Ombres errantes*.'

CHAPTER 50

The strand of time can be situated in the world:

 It lies between the erstwhile and death.

 Oe wrote to Narumi:

 I hasten

 Along the little stretch of path

 Left uncovered by the tide.

CHAPTER 51

On the River That Flows into the Flowers

Flowers live only by the year. A sap rises in men that reaches beyond the seasons. It is the past that carries them downstream. Flowers are without a past: they are even without season. Their sap *is* sap. They draw on the Erstwhile in action.

The sap that rises, grows, pulsates in plants and men is the time that matters to time.

Time as first, as *Primum Tempus*, time as first time, time as last time, time as melancholy and as mortal—these things exist only for human societies.

The Erstwhile, sprouting and growth, the instinctual act, burrowing, bounding, flying—animals all *are*, without having to know that they are.

On every animal face there is something aged. An air of the Erstwhile.

Time as springtime is something invented by human beings.

Springtime as something beautiful in girls and boys was invented by men.

*

We come from water, since we come from the sea. We are descended first from bacteria. Then we are descended from the apes.

Between the bacteria and the apes there were the fish. The carps that live four times as long as we do.

At the ends of our fingers a few scales remain.

We too derive from the stars and the sun.

All men and mountains, all flowers, all fish, all carps, all towns, all musical instruments, all apes, all books, all our faces revolve around the sun.

*

Where did this retrospective mania come from that I have deep inside me, this mania that was not concerned with the self—nor even with the imprint received from a language and a civilization—but had opened itself up forever to what is most distant?

As though unlocked to the most distant of things? Given over to pure perception? Abandoned to that attention that forgets the meaning of what it sees and loses time at the same time as it loses language?

Whence this taste for the odour of the past and the lustre of the erstwhile, which, far from wearying, have always thrilled me wherever I've been in this world?

*

The past flows from the strange expansion that *is* this world.

Life is this exuberant colonization of the slightest fragment, the tiniest fissure.

I raised my eyes.

For every living creature, to contemplate the sky, which is not alive, is to contemplate the only ancestor.

*

The background radiation of love,

the radiation within us of the ante-human way mammals have of coupling and reproducing,

the background radiation of sperm,

of milk,

of the wave that breaks on the brown shore at the sea's edge,

are the most affecting of the attractions driving human beings,

Of sperm from which an invisible scene is made.

*

We speak of the current of a river, of its *running*. What would the *run* of the river be? The *run* would be the spring just before it spurted forth. It would be the lost element that returns in the to-come of the coming that is lost. To the word *present* we ought to prefer the more certain word *passing*. The present is the passing of time. But I doubt this. I doubt that the passing of time is its source. It is possible that, in the passing of time, the past is the energy (the kernel, the black hole that lies at the heart of the afflux, that unleashes the flow). Just as the word *current* says something deeper than all the water in the river.

Other resurgences correspond to that of groundwater. The connection to a more ancient past also enables intra-terrestrial fire to erupt.

Or water, as it thaws, makes way in the cliffs for the caves, bears, eagles and men who supplanted each other there in their ways and customs, their furs, their plumage.

Men need a past in order that the passing may pass.

This night needs a dawn. This conflict needs a persecutor. This wait needs a hero. A lost-but-returning spring is needed to orient this world. A celestial chariot is needed to soothe this darkening of the night. The selfsame question leads the selfsame antediluvian answer to well up. This is myth. The past is a pile of answers: a flood.

The past is the answer piling up.

Time is questioning spurting forth.

I have made my pilgrimages around the earth. Not for accumulations of past but for signs of the Erstwhile.

We are poor riddles. The riddle is the question that calls for the answer that built it. The answer that built it is past. The guesser knows that the answer is always the past.

*

In Old High German, the word for riddle was *tunkal*, which I can translate as the shadowy thing, the oppressive thing, the thing that plunges the mind into darkness, that dooms the mind to a despairing quest, to an inquiry all the more humiliating for the fact that there is a preceding solution, a solution preceding the person's life and he is incapable of knowing where to look for it since he is alive.

The riddle speaks only of the scene that precedes life among the living.

It represses the scene of animals coupling.

It embellishes that scene, while preventing it from being seen.

Everything in the paradoxical, twisted, contorted, impossible way the question of the riddle is couched is done to disrupt the quest and render its object invisible.

It is probable that the echo of language in the mind (in consciousness) forces us to believe in the truth of riddles. But it is possible that the right question is merely an invention. It is possible that every human narrative is a myth unrelated to the events of one's own life, but that the possibility of narration alone renders that life bearable. We need a name for the anonymous.

All lives are false.

It is narration that is alive, or vital, or vitalizing, or revivifying.

It is possible that novelists are the only ones to know the error engendered by all narration—since they devote their time to working on its errancy—and the strange vitality that arises out of that fiction. The only ones to know that there are so many possible novels and no truth whatever upstream from them. That there are so many possible questions and no riddle really underlying every drama advancing within them.

This is why human beings are so fond of taking examinations, competing for qualifications, undergoing initiations or elections, why they enter so many competitions, read so many mystery novels, inexplicably enjoy doing crosswords: they wish to believe there is a response that precedes their question, where there is, in fact, only pulmonation, an invisible scene, an aimless bodily questioning, a sexual contingency. They want to believe there is an initial ciphering, that there is some direction or promise to their days.

Everyone wants to believe that there are keys for the jammed, groaning, rusty locks each person has become. That a password can grant us entry to a group and we can thereby avoid the sacrificial death constantly in preparation there, with its accompanying trumpeting or lowing of the herd, its unavowed collective jubilation. That some string-pulling can get the social machine moving again, when it is merely a scaffold and a burial mound. That a zodiac animal has influence, that a god exists who takes us from darkness to sunlight, that the night can be deciphered and there is a voice that orders human chaos when it is mouldering away into death.

CHAPTER 52

Like a blind man recovering his sight, like a deaf one hearing again, like a prisoner emerging from his exile, they come back, they arrive, they look, but it is hardly the kingdom that they rediscover. You leave the century and arrive at time. You leave the nation and arrive at a place. You leave your name behind and arrive at the semi-animality of desire and the demi-humanity of nascent language. I was becoming less and less proud and more and more distant.

The distant, the distended, the temporal is the separate.

*

The lost defines the elsewhere (*In aliore loco*).

*

The detached element is almost free.

*

After leaving for Rome at the age of fourteen to learn how to paint, Monsieur Marc Antoine Charpentier returned from that city a musician.

His head had been turned by the airs composed in those times by Signor Carissimi.[†]

One fine day he abandoned the visible.

He gave up the north-facing window lights of the painters' studios.

*

Having closed the blinds and pulled the hook towards him, he sat down in the shadows. Between the wooden shutter and the harpsichord, he said:

'I've already forgotten the eyelids that are raised and opened wide to see. Gone from my memory are the dresses and wonderful scents that surround the young women and are borne around by them. Forgotten are the galleys casting off in the distance and the dazzling sunlight falling on the tiny oars and the tiny sailors. I compose lessons in darkness for candles I extinguish. I hear ghostly lamentations of dying gods.'

CHAPTER 53

The Other Kingdom

In 1602, a master fisherman in the Morbihan region of the province of Brittany, owned five boats. He had been three years a widower, not having remarried, so much did the love for the woman who had been his wife endure within him. His house was built on the cliffside. The coast on which it was situated was a coast of black rocks. The path leading to it was steep. The house was narrow and the rooms dark. He was eating his gruel.

Through the house door he saw his wife pass by. He dropped his bowl and ran out on to the path that fell away precipitously towards the sea.

She wore a tapering white linen bodice above a buttercup yellow skirt.

'Have you not been dead these three years?' he shouted.

His wife, with little nods of her head, concurred in this. By her side stood the former village minstrel.

He seemed much younger than she did.

In actual fact, he had predeceased her by nine years.

He stood back from her a way. He too was dressed in yellow linen. He looked serious. He seemed lost in thought.

While the widower spoke to his dead wife, the minstrel sat on a rock. He had in his hands a large, steel-tipped cane.

A traveller arrived, coming from the Scorff river, and went by.

As he was passing, he greeted them in the English tongue.

The minstrel replied, likewise in English.

The minstrel and the master fisherman's wife were both dressed in linen, as are all the dead.

They were very handsome, though their cheeks were white and hollow.

'In truth, you did not love those whom you loved after this man?' said the master fisherman to his wife at this point.

'No.'

'You didn't love me?'

'No.'

'You always preferred a dead man to a living one?'

'Yes.'

'Why?'

The woman made no reply.

'Tell me why,' the fisherman insisted.

'No.'

After refusing to reply, the dead wife turned her back on him. She made ready to carry on down the path.

Her face was extraordinarily luminous.

The minstrel also got up, using his cane for support.

The master-fisherman rushed forward.

The dead woman bent double, gathered up her skirts and began to run along the precipitous path.

But the master-fisherman, grabbing hold of a stem of broom and leaping on to an overhanging rock, managed to get beyond her.

The widower howled.

He shook his fists. He wept too.

He prevented his dead wife from passing.

The cliff top was so narrow at this point that had the dead woman fallen, she would have injured herself or, at least, would have spoilt her linen clothing.

The wife remained stockstill before he former husband.

The master-fisherman begged her one last time:

'If you'll explain to me why you didn't love me as much as the minstrel, I'll let you pass.'

She looked him in the eyes.

Then she shrugged her shoulders.

She turned to gaze out to sea.

After this, she gave her husband another long look. Her expression was not contemptuous, but there was no tenderness in it either.

She lowered her eyelids but said nothing.

Softly he said: 'Tell me, my love, why you no longer love me?'

His wife's beautiful face was, at this point, to his left. He saw her in profile. He did not see her lips move. Yet he heard her say in a quiet voice:

'I found more pleasure in the company of this dead man, even for a minute, even in thought, even in endlessly chewing over in my mouth the secret of his name, than in ten years in your arms, even when I was happy in your arms.'

'Ah!' he sighed, and he collapsed on the ground.

They passed him by.

They went down the path.

They reached the sand and the beach. They held hands beside the waves.

They walked on the seaweed right at the bottom.

The fisherman could see their yellow clothing floating above the seaweed and the pools of water.

He was jealous.

Though both were dead, the master-fisherman was jealous of their happiness among the dead.

He returned home in a dreadful state.

The master-fisherman was in constant suffering, not because his wife was now a ghost, but because in the other world she had preferred a man to whom she had given herself before she had met him. He said:

'I wish it on no one to see who it is that the dead choose to love.'

Often, after saying these words, he added with a threatening air towards his listeners:

'And I don't wish any of you to discover who it is that is loved by those with whom you live!'

They say his suffering lasted six months, until the month of April.

It is a strange kingdom I evoke here to open these volumes—these heathlands, these white waves, this yellow broom, these cliffs.

Strips of seaweed, bits of seashell, wrecked boats, seashores, fragments of invisible scenes.

On 23 April his tears at last began to flow. He began to eat again. He had been refusing to sleep because he feared his wife might appear to him in his dreams. Despite all that had happened, he was afraid he might desire her in his sleep. He had lost six and a half stones.

CHAPTER 54

There was a kingdom of Jerusalem that was French.

It lasted less than a man's lifetime.

In 1203 it did not exist.

By 1262 it was finished.

In going to the Crusades, in going to Asia, the knights were going in search of tales.

CHAPTER 55

Sofiius' End

I have not told the story of the end of Sofiius, secretary (*notarius*) to the last of the Romans. Admittedly, we know nothing of that end, so I shall invent it. The day after the Battle of Soissons, when Synagrius fled before the army of Clovis and Ragnacaire as far as the Visigothic court of Toulouse, Sofiius waited for his master. He watched scrupulously over his library. In the evening he took a boat on to the Aisne, passing down through the marble arch. Then, as night fell, he came back up towards the alabaster castle. When the population of Soissons learned Syagrius had, on Clovis' orders, been executed, after first having his head shaved, and when they found out he had expired with the enigmatic words 'Where are the shadows?' on his lips, they turned to Sofiius, but Sofiius said nothing.

The crowd withdrew.

He waited.

One day, he saw a scholar arrive from Alaric's court, a man he knew. He offered him a seat at the window bench in the library and sent for wine and a piece of dried bacon. The learned man in his turn reported the words Syagrius had spoken as he died.

He, too, asked him what was meant by these *umbrae* (shadows)?

'Those are the shadows out there,' replied Sofiius.

And he pointed out of the window.

To the west, two tall, ancient oaks were visible, filling the castle courtyard with shade.

He explained that it was the pleasure of the king of the Romans every summer's evening, when he got out of his scalding-hot bath, to sit in the shade of the oaks with him and with others, as Virgil's shepherds had done, and rest, or drink cool red wine or recite the old poems.

They fell silent. They looked through the window at the oaks and the little children playing with a rag ball in the courtyard. Sofiius the Notary went on:

'When you have eaten and drunk, we shall go and take a look at these humid shadows, if you wish.'

The scholar from Toulouse nodded and drank.

They got up, left the room and went out into the courtyard. 'Nothing is more pleasurable,' they said to one another, 'than to take a walk as evening falls. It isn't just the vault of the sky, but one's head too that is darker, more obscure. And one's calves feel numb.'

'I have no money. Would you mind making me a gift of a few bronze coins?'

Sofiius the Notary said it would be done. The scholar from Toulouse had used the old word, *stips*. He went on:

'I'm going to Trier. It would be better if you didn't stay here but came with me.'

'I think the same.'

'King Clodovecchus has chosen Soissons as his capital and will return here.'

'The old temples are not in his heart. He prefers basilicas. He loves crosses.'

'And ewers.'

'They say that he loves ewers. The world has changed.'

They had reached the oak trees and sat down on the moss that grew in their shade.

There were bees buzzing around.

'What use are these bees that poison us and sting our cheeks?' asked the scholar from Toulouse all of a sudden.

'They make honey,' replied Sofiius the Notary.

What is the use of trees so tall that when we look up at the tops of them from down here, as I'm doing now, we feel genuinely dizzy?'

'They give shade,' replied Sofiius the Notary.

'They're so tall, they're a threat to the courtyard. Moreover, they couldn't be cut down without endangering the courtyard walls.'

'That's why they are still growing. They always will. They will grow under the walls, and the stones that are dislodged will bring down the walls. The trees that cannot be used by spear carriers, makers of palissades, chariot builders, lute makers or boat builders know the exuberant utility of useless things. Virgil took refuge in their shade, as have the cool of springtime, the bees that trouble you, people doing nothing, scholars, those who touch one another when they have had a little bit to drink, the dead, fruits, children, frogs, snails, the arts, I and you.

'If the dead have no existence at all, the living don't have much more,' mumbled the man from Toulouse. 'All they need, more or less, is a bowl of gruel each day, a corner of a wall, a patch of light and a book.'

'The dead would find you ungrateful. My master is going to think I lack perseverance,' said Sofiius the Notary. 'You talk too much nonsense. You will go to Trier alone. I shall make my way to Paris.'

When night had fallen, they went into the palace. Sofiius counted out some bronze coins and the scholar set out in the moonlight.

Two days later, Sofiius himself set off. He took four books with him in scroll form: *De rerum natura* by Titus Lucretius Carus, the novels of Albucius Silus, the books of the *Metamorphoseon* of Publius Ovidius and Tacitus' *Annals*.

He followed the Aisne as far as the Oise, where he took a boat to the hills of Paris. He rented a little house on the edge of the forest, overlooking the city and the temples of Julian. He had a table to read at and he lived on stewed fruits. He planted a vine, which he later abandoned. He read out loud. He had a hunter make him a sloping roof, beneath which he placed a cistern to store the rainwater. The inhabitants of Paris came up to see him. Citizens asked him to teach their children how to shape the numbers and draw the old letters. He taught two little girls and eight little boys. In exchange for the lessons he gave their children, the parents offered him pieces of game, fish and old amphoras of wine, of which he was fond.

He had ten years of peace. One night, in 497, the man from Toulouse knocked on his door. Sofiius lit a candle. He asked him in, embraced him and poured him a bowl of old wine.

'Ah, there you are, chatterbox!' he said to him.

The man from Toulouse, his beard all dishevelled, warned him in hurried tones that the king was looking for him. Memories of Rome were to be scattered to the winds. Its very language was to be wiped out, because having been the tongue of the pagans meant that it was now the language of demons.

Sofiius was already aware of the vows the Merovingian king had sworn at the Battle of

Tolbiac.[†] He put down his earthenware bowl. He spoke the name of Constantine and talked of the dream he had dreamt and interpreted so curiously.

The source of all the trouble was that dream in which the Greek letter *tau* had been so prominent.

'The letter *chi*,' said the man from Toulouse.

'The letter *iota*,' said Sofiius.

'I'm heading south,' the man from Toulouse told him. 'I'm going back to the sun that shines over the sea in the middle of the world.'

Sofiius shook his head but said not a word.

The man from Toulouse stated that his back and his finger joints could no longer stand the Gaulish climate and that fear had seized him, together with a yearning for the sun. They spoke together of ancient scholars and quoted anecdotes that filled them each with delight. When he was himself very young and learning his declamations, the scholar from Toulouse had known an old woman who boasted of having fellated Augustine at Milan in the days when he was still a pagan. He had also known Olybrius and he praised his seriousness and virtue, as well as the grave sadness of his death.

'Mention of the old times makes people very sad,' said Sofiius. 'We should think of leaving.'

'Will you go with me to Rome?'

'I find no pleasure in contemplating ruins. I'm not a philosopher. I seek long life and the pleasure of the hours. I shall go to Rheims.'

'You're mad. The Franks are looking for you.'

'Life has wearied me. The light has burned my eyes. I enjoyed talking with Syagrius. The proximity of death is perhaps more of a living thing than a life devoted to fleeing it. I should have liked to have given the last king the old ritual of the ashes that are borne on the air and ascend until they blend with the transparency of the element in which our faces bathe and where cries and babies are born. It is at the heart of the storm that we sometimes find the bosom of peace and gentleness. I have no wish to be endlessly on the move now, to be concealing my life. I dread listlessness and anxiety. I've thrown aside the tablet and the stylus the way little fresh, quivering butterflies slough off their casings. There will be no sages left in the universe if they all carry on running. If all the sages flee, how will the temples follow them? I shall put the mask of the approaching cloud on my face, because the other side of the cloud is always in the sun. What use is there in being afraid? What use is there in galloping like the barbarians who invade this land that has already been invaded a hundred times before? My body will be a little fragmentary book that my breath will read as it leaves it. The shadows will preserve a memory of my dreams and will lengthen. My medicine chest and the memory of beauty will keep me company. I shall take a boy or caress a woman silently, without my lips being sullied by the words of the Upper Rhine. At the moment when the enemy lies in wait for me, I'll uncross my knees and go to the kitchen to pour myself a bowl of wine and put it on the stove to warm; I'll dip my piece of crust in it.'

Sofiius offered his books to the man from Toulouse, but he declined them, white with fear. He admitted he feared being killed if they were found among his luggage. The Christians weren't people to be fooled with. They bade each other farewell, since they knew they would not see one another again before they died, clasping each other by the forearm, as men of old did on the banks of the Tiber, men who would brook no servitude.

After the man from Toulouse had left, Sofiius burned those of Syagrius' books that he had brought with him, after twice reciting each of them to himself.

He then did as he said he would. King Clovis had outlawed all memory of the pagans and he masked his face. He turned himself into a monk. He went to Rheims.

In the basilica, during the service, he clasped his fingers together and recited, deep within himself, the adventures of Orpheus anxiously climbing his rocky path while keeping his eyes fixed straight ahead. Or the legend of Echo turned to stone. His face gave nothing away. He had a protuberant forehead. His freedom was indomitable. He never opened his mouth and nothing could betray his thoughts. His brothers said he was so close to God that he forgot to cross himself. Not only did they not come near him, they also maintained a zone of silence and avoidance around him.

He drank a peck of wine each day. Then two pecks. His advice was attentively heeded, since he never opened his mouth and confined himself to nodding or shaking his head.

He had no sorrows. He breathed gently, expelling the air noiselessly. He was seen as a modest man, a saint, his eyes always lowered to the ground. He didn't greatly like contemplating the idol hanging on the wall, which evoked death for him, and he was at pains to understand how a people that boasted of its freedom had chosen a tortured, suffering slave as an image of omnipotence and happiness. He would go into the courtyard, crouch down against the trees and sit there with his eyes open in their shade. They sometimes saw his lips moving.

He was still alive when Theodoric had Boethius beheaded.[†] He died in 533 at Rheims in the shade of an elm tree in the close surrounding the basilica. He fell suddenly, having fallen asleep on his feet as he left the kitchens. He was mourned by his brother monks with chants in his memory. The pontiff Remigius survived him by twelve days.

TRANSLATOR'S NOTES

Chapter 1

Larvatus, said Descartes . . . Descartes' full statement was '*Ut comædi, moniti ne in fronte appareat pudor, personam induunt, sic ego hoc mundi teatrum conscensurus, in quo hactenus spectator exstiti, larvatus prodeo.*' See C. Adam and P. Tannery (eds), *Oeuvres de Descartes* (Paris: Vrin, 1974), pp. *x*, 213.

On 31 March 1649 . . . Descartes, *Oeuvres et Lettres* (Paris: Gallimard, Collection La Pléiade, 1953) has a slightly different version of the text of this letter at p. 1331. There, Descartes suggests they want him '*comme un éléphant ou un panthère, à cause de la rareté, et non point pour y être utile à quelque chose*' (as an elephant or a panther, for reasons of rarity, and not to be useful for something).

Chapter 2

The sixth book of the Chin P'ing Mei . . . *The Plum in the Golden Vase or, Chin P'ing Mei* is currently being translated by David Tod Roy for Princeton University Press. The first three volumes have appeared so far.

Three golden hairs . . . 'The Devil with the Three Golden Hairs', one of the traditional tales collected and retold by the Brothers Grimm.

This expression, simple as it is ... The passage is from Petronius, *Satiricon* 129.

Chapter 4

Your step began to totter ... The first words of this paragraph are taken from St Jerome's *Letters* (Eusebius Hieronymus Sophronius, *Epistolae* 5, 147), while the latter part is from *De Lapsis* (*On the Apostates* or *On the Lapsed*) by St Cyprien of Carthage (Cyprianus Carthaginensis).

Jean-Baptiste Massillon . . . Jean-Baptiste Massillon (1663–1742) was a French Catholic bishop and a famous pulpit orator. He was Bishop of Clermont from 1717 to 1742.

Chapter 5

Antoine Arnauld and Pierre Nicole ... Antoine Arnauld (1612–94), French Catholic theologian, philosopher and mathematician, was one of the leading intellectuals of the Jansenists of Port-Royal. Pierre Nicole (1625–95), theologian and philosopher, co-authored with Arnauld the *Port Royal Logic* (1662) and *La Perpétuité de la foi de l'Église catholique touchant l'eucharistie* (1669).

Rancé wrote to Retz ... Armand Jean Le Bouthillier de Rancé (1626–1700) was a monk and a distinguished scholar. Jean François Paul de Gondi, Cardinal de Retz (1613–79) was a leading French churchman and memoirist.

Chapter 7

In 395 . . . Martin of Tours (316–97) was acclaimed bishop of Tours in 371 CE. Saint Brice (Bricius; *c.*370–444), who is said to have been rescued as an orphan by Martin, later became Martin's pupil and succeeded him as bishop in 397 CE.

Chapter 8

A pontiff, also from Tours . . . The reference is to Gregory of Tours (*c.*538–94), who tells Syagrius' story in his *History of the Franks*. He was bishop of Tours from 573 CE until his death.

Clovis marched against him . . . Clovis (also known as Chlodwig, Chlodowech or Chlodovecchus; *c.*466–511) was king first of the Salian Franks, then of all the Franks from 481 to 511 CE. His reign is recorded in Gregory of Tours' *History of the Franks* and he is generally regarded as the first Christian ruler of the Frankish kingdom. Ragnacaire was the Frankish king of Cambrai in present-day northern France. He and his two brothers, Riquier and Renomer (aka Rignomer, Ragnomer and Richomer) were taken prisoner and executed by Clovis.

We are not speaking here . . . Saints Crispin and Crispinian (Shakespeare's Crispin Crispian), twin brothers of noble Roman birth, were martyred at Soissons in 286 CE. Having made shoes by night and preached by day, they became the patron saints of cobblers and of leather workers in general.

In 451 Attila had spared Soissons . . . Attila (*c.*406–53) was the king of the Hunnic tribes, peoples from a region stretching from

Eastern Europe to the steppes of Central Asia. According to Roman historiography, his reign extended from 434 CE to his death.

It was during this campaign ... The vases Clovis had removed are generally thought to have been all those that made reference to the Romans.

Chapter 9

It is a gilded ewer ... The story of the ewer of Soissons (also known as the vase of Soissons) is told by Gregory of Tours in *History of the Franks*. See Gregory of Tours, *The History of the Franks* (Harmondsworth: Penguin, 1974), BK 2, CHAP. 27, pp. 139–40.

Where the Elysian Fields ... Cumae is probably best known as the seat of the Cumaean Sibyl. In Greek mythology, Erebus was the son of the primordial god Chaos and was the personification of darkness and shadow. The Erinyes or Eumenides are most commonly known in English as the 'Furies' and were female deities of vengeance. Charon was the ferryman of Hades.

Chapter 10

Te loquor absentem ... The phrase is from Ovid, *Tristia ex Ponto* 3.3.17, lines written from exile at Tomis on the Black Sea.

Chapter 11

Zenchiku wrote ... Komparu Zenchiku (1405–*c*.1470) was a Japanese Noh actor, troupe leader and playwright. He lived, worked and died in the Nara area of Japan, being trained by the renowned Zeami.

Chapter 13

The fluid, golden light . . . The Yonne is a northern French river, running mainly through Burgundy and feeding into the Seine at Montereau-Fault-Yonne in Seine-et-Marne. It gives its name to the *département* that has its administrative capital at Auxerre.

Chapter 15

In 1933 Tanizaki published . . . Junichiro Tanizaki, *In Praise of Shadows* (Thomas J. Harper and Edward G. Seidensticker trans) (London: Vintage, 2001).

Chapter 16

The overripe pear, moist with juice . . . Verneuil-sur-Avre is a small French town situated in the Eure department of Upper Normandy. It is famed for the battle fought nearby in 1424 during the Hundred Years' War.

A child opening his mouth . . . Where Anglo-Saxon tradition has a tooth fairy, French children offer up their fallen teeth to *la petite souris*, the little mouse.

Chapter 18

There is in the thought of Monsieur de Saint-Cyran . . . Jean-Ambroise Duvergier de Hauranne (1581–1643) was better known as the abbé de Saint-Cyran or simply Monsieur de Saint-Cyran. He was the French monk and theologian who introduced Jansenism into France. After his arrest on Richelieu's orders, he was held in the Château de Vincennes and released only after Richelieu's death on 6 February 1643. He died shortly afterwards.

Chapter 19

He was always ready with this phrase . . . The Imitation of Christ: *De imitatione Christi* is a manual of devotion written by Thomas à Kempis. It was originally published anonymously in Latin around 1418.

Such is Lake Avernus and such . . . Lake Avernus (Lago d'Averno) is located in the Avernus volcanic crater in Campania, Southern Italy. The Romans regarded it as the entrance to Hades and the term Avernus was often used by Roman authors as synonymous with the Underworld.

Such were the boiling pitch and Cerberus . . . In Greek mythology, Cerberus (Kerberos) is the multi-headed dog guarding the gates of Hades.

Thine own nation and the chief priests . . . John 18:35.

Regnum meum non est de hoc mundo . . . John 18:36.

Si de mundo fuissetis . . . John 15:19.

Chapter 21

We are speaking here of the kingdom of Josaphat ... The story of Josaphat and Barlaam, as it appears, for example, in *The Golden Legend*, would seem to be a Christian transposition of the life of the Buddha. It appears to have passed to the West by way of a number of Georgian and Arabic versions. Josaphat (Georgian Iodasaph) is generally thought to derive from the Sanskrit term *Bodhisattva*, which implies enlightenment.

Tukaram has a phrase ... Tukaram (1608–50) was a prominent Hindu religious poet from Maharashtra, India.

Plotinus said that successive reincarnations ... The Egyptian-born philosopher Plotinus (*c.*205–70) is generally regarded as the founder of Neoplatonism.

Chapter 23

They are both ante saecula ... 'Natus ante saecula' means 'begotten before the worlds'.

Chapter 26

It was Sabina Spielrein who ... The Russian doctor Sabina Naftulovna Spielrein (1884–42) was one of the earliest female psychoanalysts. The Wednesday meeting in question was one of the sessions of the Wednesday Psychological Society, which began meeting in Freud's apartment in 1902 and later evolved into the Vienna Psychoanalytic Society.

In hac flamma ... A reference to the biblical 'Crucior in hac flamma' ('I am tormented in this flame'), Luke 16:24.

Upsurge of death ... 'Little Boy' was the code name given to the atom bomb dropped on Hiroshima on 6 August 1945.

Izumi Shikibu ... Izumi Shikibu was a Japanese poet of the Heian period. She numbers among the famous 'Thirty-Six Medieval Immortals' of Japanese poetry selected by Fujiwara no Kintō.

Chapter 27

In the wake of the Saint Bartholomew's Day Massacres ... The St Bartholomew's Day Massacres were carried out by Roman Catholics against French Protestant Huguenots over a number of weeks in August and September 1572. They were thought by some to have been instigated by Catherine de' Medici.

Chapter 29

Han Yu ... Han Yu was a major poet and essayist of the Tang dynasty and a precursor of neo-Confucianism.

Georges Bataille's The Accursed Share *is one* ... Georges Bataille, *The Accursed Share: Volumes 1* and 2 (Robert Hurley trans.) (New York: Zone Books, 1988, 1991).

Chapter 30

The Vestals at Rome ... Regarding the *fascinus*, Quignard writes, 'What the Greeks called *phallos* was called *fascinus* in Latin.' See *Sex and Terror* (Chris Turner trans.) (London, New York and Calcutta: Seagull Books, 2011).

Chapter 31

White horses are not horses . . . This (originally Chinese) phrase goes back to Gongsun Long (Kung-sun Lung) and is meant to illustrate a point not about horses but about the verb 'to be', which can mean, in this context: *is not identical with x* or *is not a subset of x*. Clearly, white horses *are* horses in the latter sense but not in the former (that is, they are not identical with *all* horses).

Chapter 33

Of the Calvinists' maxim Post tenebras lux, *I retain only the first two words* . . . 'After darkness, [the] light.' As a mark of its role in the Calvinist movement, this motto is engraved on the Mur des Réformés in Geneva.

Ernest Renan was reluctant to accept . . . Ernest Renan (1823–92) was one of the foremost French writers of the nineteenth century. He was particularly renowned in his lifetime for his controversial *Life of Jesus* (1863).

Similarly, Émile Auguste Chartier wrote pieces in the Dépêche de Rouen *without taking any payment for them* . . . Chartier (1868–1951), better known by the soubriquet Alain, taught philosophy for many years at the Lycée Henri-IV in Paris, where his pupils included such luminaries as Raymond Aron, Simone Weil and Georges Canguilhem.

The templum *of Juno Moneta was filled with sounds of the smiths hammering* . . . The Temple of Juno Moneta, built in fulfilment of a vow made by Lucius Furius Camillus during the war against the Auruncii, was built on the Arx Capitolina in Rome in 344 BCE.

Chapter 36

The mysterious sermon . . . A single sermon is attributed to the *Barfüsser Lesemeister* in the Dominican collection *Paradisus anime intelligentis*. Its author is traditionally regarded as having been active in the first half of the fourteenth century. A *Lesemeister* was a man authorized to teach theology in the early modern university and I have therefore rendered the French *lecteur aux pieds nus* as 'barefoot teacher': more literally, Quignard's French expression means, of course, a barefoot *reader*.

Chapter 37

Terror . . . This is the Latin word *terror*, meaning fright, terror, dread.

In 1936, Thierry Maulnier founds Combat . . . Thierry Maulnier was the *nom de plume* of Jacques Talagrand (1908–88), a prominent journalist and writer of the French extreme Right in the interwar years, associated with the Action française movement and newspaper. After the Second World War, he was known largely as a playwright, essayist and critic, contributing regularly to the mainstream right-wing newspaper *Le Figaro*. Robert Brasillach (1909–45) was a contemporary of Maulnier's at the École normale supérieure. For his vociferous advocacy of fascism and anti-Semitism in the 1930s, particularly in the columns of *Je suis partout*, and his subsequent collaborationism, he was executed by firing squad at the Liberation.

Claude Orland . . . Claude Roy (1915–97) originally wrote under the pen name Claude Orland, under which guise he contributed several literary articles to the fascistic weekly *Je suis partout*. He joined the French resistance in 1941 and the Communist Party in 1943. After the war, he came to be known largely as a poet, novelist and essayist.

Maurice Blanchot publishes a long article . . . Maurice Blanchot (1907–2003) was a novelist, literary critic and philosopher who also flirted with the extreme Right in this period, though, as in the case of Roy, his primary associations were largely with members of the Left in the post-war years.

Vercors: Between the occupier and the writer . . . This is a reference to the novel *Le silence de la mer* by Jean Bruller (1902–91) who wrote under the pen name 'Vercors'. The book is available in English in a translation by Cyril Connolly entitled *Put out the Light* (London: Macmillan, 1944).

Chapter 39

La Fontaine's Fables met with immediate favour . . . Jean de La Fontaine (1621–95) was the most famous French fabulist of his day and is one of France's great classical poets.

St Thomas used the word abalietas . . . The reference is to the scholastic philosopher and theologian Saint Thomas Aquinas (1225–74). While *ens a se*, being in oneself, belongs to the

Creator, *ens ab alio* (*abalietas*) is the form of being that is proper to created beings.

Regina rerum oratio ... As quoted by Cicero (*De Oratore* 2.44), the phrase runs: '*Omnium Regina rerum oratio*'—literally, 'Oratory is the queen of all things.'

Chapter 41

Rousseau had a friend ... The town of Soleure in Switzerland is known as Solothurn in German.

Chapter 42

She sat in a brouette . . . In the eighteenth century, a *brouette* was a wheeled sedan chair, also called a *berouette* or *vinaigrette*. The modern word *brouette* has come to mean a garden wheelbarrow.

Chapter 43

Everything the dead man is supposed to have been fond of ... These lines are quoted from Caesar, *The Conquest of Gaul* (S. A. Handford trans.) (Harmondsworth: Penguin, 1975) p. 35.

In this Urszene *full of images* ... The Freudian term *Urszene* is normally translated into English as 'primal scene'.

Chapter 44

Yao handed on the state to Shun who passed it to Yu ... Yao (2357–2257 BCE) was succeeded by Shun as ruler of China.

Yu the Great, chosen by Shun as his successor, founded the first Xia (or Hsia) dynasty (2205 BCE).

Chapter 45

I don't want them to take me to Drancy ... The Drancy internment camp (1941–44) on the outskirts of Paris was used to hold Jews and other 'undesirables' who were to be deported to the Nazi concentration camps from Vichy France.

Chapter 46

The Augustinus appeared ... The *Augustinus* of Cornelius Jansen or, to give it its original title, *Augustinus, seu doctrina S. Augustini de humanae naturae sanitate, aegritudine, medicina, adversus Pelagianos et Massilienses* (Louvain, 1640) was Jansen's exposition of the doctrine of St Augustine on grace and predestination that famously gave rise to the 'Jansenist controversy' in seventeenth century France.

We withdraw into gardens of eighty mines: The *mine* appears to have been a measure of land on the basis of its potential yield.

Chapter 47

When, in the summer of 1824: The reference to 'a grave-looking fellow' occurs in Bonnell Collection (MS 80 [11]), Bronte Parsonage Museum, Haworth, West Yorkshire.

I have never seen [my sister's] parallel in anything. Stronger than a man, simpler than a child, her nature stood alone ... and *She made haste to leave us . . .* These words are taken directly from Charlotte Bronte's 'Biographical Notice of Acton and Ellis Bell' that appeared in the combined 1850 edition of her sisters' works *Wuthering Heights* and *Agnes Grey*.

Chapter 48

In 212 BCE, under the emperor Qin Shi-huang . . . Qin Shi-huang, formerly king of Qin during the so-called Warring States period, became the first emperor of a unified China in 221 BCE.

Damascius at Baghdad learned Pahlavi . . . Damaskios or Damascius, who lived from the mid-fifth to mid-sixth centuries CE, was one of the pagan philsophers persecuted by Justinian in the early sixth century. He is sometimes known as 'the last of the Neoplatonists'.

Chapter 49

He loved the rustic appearance of this abode . . . Flavius Claudius Julianus (*c.*331–63), commonly known as Julian, was Roman emperor from 355 to 363. Though a member of the Constantinian dynasty, he rejected Christianity in favour of Neoplatonism and is often referred to, as a consequence, as Julian the Apostate.

He resided in the former palace of Constantius Chlorus . . . Also known as Flavius Valerius Constantius or Constantius I, Constantius Chlorus (250–306); father of Constantine the Great.

239

They contained trees from the time of Camulogenus ... A Celtic general at the battle of Lutetia (present-day Paris) in 52 BCE.

Chapter 52

His head had been turned by the airs composed ... Giacomo Carissimi (1605–74) was one of the most celebrated Italian composers of the early Baroque.

Chapter 55

Sofiius was already aware of the vows ... The Battle of Tolbiac (or Zülpich, which is widely assumed by current historians to be the site of the encounter) was fought between the Franks and the Alamanni in 496 CE. Clovis is said by Gregory of Tours to have vowed to convert to Christianity if he was favoured with victory against the Alamanni.

He was still alive when Theodoric had Boethius beheaded ... The Christian philosopher Anicius Manlius Severinus Boethius, author of *The Consolation of Philosophy*, was executed by Theodoric the Great in or around 525 CE.